"I can keep you safe..."

Vince turned her onto her stomach. His hands went to work, starting with her neck. He massaged every muscle, trailing kisses down her naked back as he went.

"Kate?" He continued to work his wonders as he whispered, "Do you know what I am?"

"What?" she asked dreamily, sinking into the pillow.

"I'm a detective. I live to uncover mysteries. And you...I don't know the first thing about you."

She stiffened. *Please not now.* Not when she was so happy.

His hand ran up her spine so softly, she shivered. "I don't suppose I'll ever get my answers." His lips moved closer to her ear. "But here's the weird part. I don't give a damn."

She sighed with gratitude and thanks. Turning over, she opened her arms, and he came to her. They simply hugged. With their bodies touching all the way down.

When Kate moved it was in invitation. She pulled him close with her legs, centered him with a shift of her hips. He entered her with the same patience he'd used on her muscles. In this, there was no mystery. None at all.

Blaze™

Dear Reader,

In my last Harlequin Blaze novel, *Closer...* you met six exciting characters who now set the stage for a brand-new miniseries launching this month called IN TOO DEEP.... It's about people who fight for truth and justice and fall in love along the way.

In *Relentless*, Kate Rydell is working at a hotel, trying to stay out of sight. But when she witnesses a murder, all hell breaks loose. Detective Vince Yarrow must take her into protective custody. They learn what I believe is the best lesson of all: that while we can (and do) tackle the tough stuff alone, it's infinitely easier when we have someone we love by our side. Of course, it takes them a while to see that they're better together than apart. But getting there is incredibly...interesting.

In January look for *Release*, Seth and Harper's story, followed in March by *Reckoning* where Nate and Tam meet again, with sizzling consequences.

I hope you enjoy the IN TOO DEEP... miniseries. Please visit my Web site at www.joleigh.com.

Best,

Jo Leigh

RELENTLESS
Jo Leigh

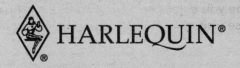

HARLEQUIN®

TORONTO • NEW YORK • LONDON
AMSTERDAM • PARIS • SYDNEY • HAMBURG
STOCKHOLM • ATHENS • TOKYO • MILAN • MADRID
PRAGUE • WARSAW • BUDAPEST • AUCKLAND

ISBN-13: 978-0-373-79293-1
ISBN-10:   0-373-79293-X

RELENTLESS

Copyright © 2006 by Jolie Kramer.

This edition published by arrangement with Harlequin Books S.A.

® and TM are trademarks of the publisher. Trademarks indicated with
® are registered in the United States Patent and Trademark Office, the
Canadian Trade Marks Office and in other countries.

www.eHarlequin.com

Printed in U.S.A.

ABOUT THE AUTHOR

Jo Leigh has written over thirty books for Harlequin and Silhouette Books since 1994. She's a double RITA® Award finalist, and was part of the exciting Harlequin Blaze launch. She also teaches writing in workshops across the country.

Jo lives in Utah with her wonderful husband and their new puppy, Jessie. You can chat with her at her Web site, www.joleigh.com, and don't forget to check out her daily blog!

Books by Jo Leigh

Don't miss any of our special offers. Write to us at the following address for information on our newest releases.

Harlequin Reader Service
U.S.: 3010 Walden Ave., P.O. Box 1325, Buffalo, NY 14269
Canadian: P.O. Box 609, Fort Erie, Ont. L2A 5X3

This one is for Barbara Joel,
with love and gratitude.

1

KATE SHOULD HAVE kept her eyes on her job, restocking the little refrigerator behind the bar, but she was so bored it was hard not to look around. All day, five days a week, pushing her cart in and out of rooms, checking how many little bottles of vodka, bourbon or gin had been used, how many candy bars and packets of peanuts had been nibbled. It was ridiculous that she had to spend so many hours doing this, while she should be putting all her energy into getting her life back.

Unfortunately, she needed to eat and she preferred a roof over her head. So she worked for room service at the Meridian Hotel in downtown Los Angeles. Laying low, staying as invisible as possible.

Kate preferred empty rooms where she was able to sail in and out quickly with her cart, ignoring the bland decor, identical in every room, down to the tan-colored, easy-to-disinfect imitation leather upholstery.

She shuddered at the memory of the couple in 1242 on Monday afternoon who'd forgotten to hang out the Do Not Disturb card or bolt the door. She'd walked in on them having wild sex on top of the bedspread. Kate had just muttered her apologies and left, conveniently forgetting to return before the end of her shift. Undoubtedly the hotel manager would have docked her wages if they'd complained, but they hadn't.

At least this guest, a nice-looking man in his thirties who'd barely acknowledged her when she'd come in, had stayed in the suite's living room. At first she'd thought he was talking to her, then she'd realized he was rehearsing a speech. One part of a speech. Something to do with changing neighborhoods for the better.

She tried again to concentrate on her job as the man paced across the room. She still had six more suites on this floor to do before lunch and couldn't afford to have her pay docked. She just wished the job was more interesting. It left her with way too much time to think. To be afraid.

She looked up, not at the man, but at the mirror behind the bar, and saw him cross the room. She'd grown accustomed to being on the alert, always conscious of any and all entrances and exits. It had taken time to grasp that nowhere was safe, but she got it now. Behind every door, every smile, lay the potential for danger.

There was a knock at the door just as she crouched down to stock the fridge. The mirror gave her a clear view of the room, while the bar hid her from sight. She stilled, trying to convince herself it was probably nothing. Room service. A friend. Not about her at all. Then she smiled at her own paranoia. There were two sodas and a couple of candy bars missing, and she reached into her cart to dig out the replacements.

The guest opened the door, not cautiously as she would have, but calmly intent. Two young men, both Asian, dressed in baggy clothes with hoodies under their coats, rushed in. The guest cried out and tried to block them. Before Kate could even reach for the gun in her ankle holster, the men drew their automatic weapons. Gunfire exploded, and she watched as the guy was torn apart, his blood seeping into the pale carpet.

Terrified, she held her breath, knowing she wouldn't stand a chance against automatic weapons, knowing this man, this nice guy practicing his speech, was dead. Was it because of her? Was *she* the real target?

The gunfire stopped and the killers left as swiftly as they had burst in. A shout echoed from the hallway; in the room though, there was nothing but quiet and the awful stench of death.

It took her a moment to realize she wasn't next. That she had to leave. This second.

She eyed her cart. There was no way she'd be able to wheel it down that hallway. Too many people had heard the gunfire. There was a fire exit just down the hall, away from the elevators. She walked to the door. Once there, she snuck a glance down the hall. There were two men, guests. They were looking around frantically, clearly reacting to the sound of the gunfire. With just two of them all she had to do was wait, and the moment they were distracted she'd make her break for the exit.

The ding from the elevator gave her her chance. The two men turned, and she was out of there. No running. Just a fast, steady walk to the fire exit door. She was on the fourteenth floor, and with every step down to the parking garage, she thought about that poor man.

Death was no stranger to her. She'd seen so many horrible things in Kosovo, where her whole universe had turned upside down. She'd been a forensic accountant, a pencil pusher. Then she'd stumbled upon a horrible secret perpetrated by her own government, and from that moment on, nothing had been the same. She'd almost been killed. Not just her, but six others who had uncovered the deadly truth. Now they were all back in the States, living under the radar, trying like hell to bring about justice and truth, all the while knowing there were men trained by the CIA who wanted them dead.

This man? This poor guy gunned down in front of her? She had no idea who he was or why those two men had killed him. The way they were dressed suggested they were gang members. The way they handled the killing made her certain of it.

Her stomach rebelled and she had to pause for a moment, breathe deeply to stop from throwing up. When she could handle it, she started down again, moving faster now, afraid that the police would see her and want to question her.

Her steps slowed as the realization sunk in—they were gangbangers. Not CIA agents. Not Omicron. Oh, God. She hadn't been their target at all. She'd just been in the wrong place at the wrong time. She would have laughed if it hadn't been so horribly tragic.

She'd witnessed a murder.

In her old life she would have stayed. She would have done everything she could to help. That wasn't possible now.

She was one of the hunted. The people who'd tried to kill her in Kosovo wanted her dead. Silenced. She'd seen things the government, her government, hadn't wanted her to see. They'd meant for her to die in a lonely warehouse in a small Serbian village. Her very existence made them vulnerable. She'd seen the lengths to which these people would go to stop her.

It would have been easier if she had money. But there was none. Not for any of them. No legitimate jobs, absolutely no using their real names. Her entire family thought she was dead.

She paused in front of the garage exit. There were probably police behind the door, and she needed to make it to her car without being spotted. The best thing she could do was act as if nothing was out of the ordinary.

There was, in fact, a police car. And an ambulance. But they weren't that close to the exit, and she had, as always, parked with an eye toward a quick getaway. Walking across the parking lot ramped up her heart rate, but the rubber soles of her shoes muffled her steps, and there was so much chatter from the cop's radio that by the time she was in her car she was pretty damn sure she was going to make it.

It occurred to her that she wasn't coming back. And that she had a full two-weeks' pay that she hadn't collected. That left her with maybe a hundred, which wasn't going to take her far.

She started her car and drove slowly to the busy downtown street. Once she reached the freeway heading toward the Valley, she started shaking.

DETECTIVE VINCE YARROW stared at the body on the floor. He tried like hell to think in terms of weapons, trajectories, points of impact, but this wasn't just another body. It was Tim Purchase, a man Vince had grown to respect and admire. A friend.

"Christ, they didn't leave much."

Vince glanced at his partner, Jeff Stoller, who looked small and weary in his heavy coat. "Just a message."

Jeff shook his head as he went over to the department photographer, there to capture the scene for the detectives and for a jury that would probably never be called.

The room was starting to get crowded, and that wouldn't do. There wasn't going to be much evidence, that much Vince knew; still he'd collect what he could. Then he would leave Tim to the coroner while he and Jeff went room to room looking for a witness.

He also knew that no one would talk. No one would admit that the perpetrators had been gangbangers. Everything about the murder screamed colors. The question was, which gang? Tim had worked against most of them, from the MS-13s, Crips and Bloods to the Aryan Nation. He'd dedicated his life to stealing kids from the gangs, to giving them opportunities to make something of themselves. He'd been a hero. A savior to hundreds. If it took him the rest of his life, Vince would catch the pricks who'd done this.

He got out his notebook and began the work. Most of the time, getting into the case soothed him. The familiar procedures helped distance him from the inhumanity of the crime. Not today. With every notation, every cold observance, his anger grew until he could feel the heat in his face and the grinding of his molars. God damn them. All of them. All the selfish little bastards who thought nothing more of murder than they thought of taking a piss.

"Vince."

He looked up from his book to find Jeff scowling. The reason was Corky Baker, a reporter for the *Times* who was a walking pain in the ass. Whenever there was a high profile murder, Baker would attach himself, leechlike, to whomever he could. Vince was all for freedom of the press and the public's right to know, though not at the victims' expense. Baker had caused him problems too many times in the past with his sleazy version of crime reporting. He owed it to Tim not to let that happen this time.

"Get him out of here." Vince looked pointedly at the bottom-feeder. "This is still an active crime scene."

Baker didn't move. "Yarrow, you never fail to enchant. I have a couple of questions—"

"Go jump off the roof."

"Can I quote you on that?"

"Jeff. Ask the officers to come in and remove Mr. Baker."

"You got it." Jeff smiled broadly at the reporter. "Should I tell them to use all necessary force?"

"Sounds good to me." Vince went back to his notebook, reading what he'd written before the interruption.

"All right, I'll go. Just tell me, was it crack? I heard Purchase was taking a hefty percentage as hush money."

Vince dropped his notebook as he crossed the room. He hit Baker so goddamned hard his head bounced off the doorframe. It wasn't nearly enough. As he moved in for round two, the bastard slid down the wall, landing in a messy heap on the floor.

Jeff stepped in front of Vince carefully. "You might have made your point there, buddy."

"Not even close."

"He's an asshole. Let it go."

Vince took in a deep breath, his body still thrumming with the need to pummel. "Get him gone, Jeff. Now."

"Why don't you go get some water, huh?"

Vince sniffed as he looked at the reporter who was just coming to. A small trickle of blood had started at the corner of his mouth, which wasn't as satisfying as one would think. The bruise would be a good one though, large and painful.

He headed for the bar, wishing he could have something a lot stronger than water. His thoughts of bourbon were interrupted by the sight of the room service cart. It was open, with all the little liquor bottles, candy bars and fruit drinks in neat order. He turned to Jeff, but cut his remark off as he saw Baker rise to his feet. The last thing Vince wanted in the paper was that there had been a witness in the room.

Baker raised his hand, swatted at the blood on his face and stared at the evidence on his fingers, then at Vince. "Thank you, you miserable prick. I'm going to sue you and your department for so much money they won't have enough left over for toilet paper. You got that?"

"Fine. Just do it somewhere else."

One of the uniforms put his hand on Baker's elbow, but he shook him off. "You'll be hearing from me."

Vince turned back to the cart. As Baker's voice receded, Vince crouched down in front of the small refrigerator. From there, he looked up into the mirror. Shit. Whoever had been here had likely seen everything. Tim opening the door. The rush inside. The blaze of bullets. They'd be able to ID the gunmen, if not by face, by colors, clothing, tattoos, headgear, weapons. It would all help him identify who'd done this. The question was, who had been behind this bar, and where were they now?

"Vince?"

"Come here, Jeff."

His partner walked over to the side of the bar. "Whoa, what have we here?"

"A witness."

"Excellent. I'll go to the manager and ask who was working."

"I'll go with you."

"I think you'd better call Emerson," Jeff said. "The second he hears about Baker's lawsuit, he's gonna blow a gasket."

Vince stood, his knee cracking with the effort. "I don't give a shit about Baker."

"You assaulted the man. He can have you arrested."

"No, he won't. He'll get more mileage from a lawsuit."

"Yeah, the Captain's gonna love that."

"I'll tell Emerson what happened. But first I need to find this witness."

Jeff, who'd been his partner for almost three years, shrugged. That's what was so good about him. He wasn't just a fine cop, he knew how to roll with the punches. And he put up with all Vince's bullshit. "I'll wait for the coroner. Come back up here when you're done."

Vince picked up his notebook on his way out, his bruised knuckles making him wince.

KATE PARKED HER beat-up Toyota in the parking lot of her apartment building. The prospect of moving again so soon after she'd found this dive made her sick. There was no choice, of course. The police could already know that she'd been in the suite during the murder. They'd be after her, and she wouldn't let herself be found.

Truthfully, it wasn't the moving that had her so edgy. It was the smell of death that was still on her, the coppery odor of blood in her hair, on her uniform. She wanted to shower, but there wouldn't be time.

She'd learned how to live in the smallest possible way. A few changes of clothes, toiletries in one tote, her computer and paperwork all in one box. She had nothing extraneous, nothing that couldn't be abandoned if she had to leave quickly. She kept the contents of her computer on a portable flash drive that was on her key ring, and she backed it up every single time she logged off. The clothes were from Goodwill, the toiletries from the dollar store. However, since last month she had one box that was more important than any of that.

A friend who'd worked with her in the forensic accounting department of the U.N. had risked his life to get photocopies of certain ledgers. Ledgers Kate had worked on in Kosovo that had given her the first inkling that all was not as it should have been.

She and Branislav had been part of the U.N.'s international war crimes tribunal, investigating ex-Yugoslav President Slobodan Milosevic and the ethnic war that had raged in the Balkans since 1986. Their specific task was to examine the hand-written ledgers from the offices of the Kosovo Liberation Army who had been accused of stealing NATO funds to pay for black market weapons.

Those ledgers had started it all. She'd found payments from the KLA to a U.S. bank. She'd assumed the KLA had found an American arms dealer, but then she'd discovered that the money had shown up in some suspicious accounts. She'd been told to leave it alone. That it wasn't important. But she'd continued to dig.

The money led her to a slush fund, which made a round-about circuit right back to the Balkans. To a laboratory run by what she now knew was a corrupt organization somehow connected to the CIA. They called themselves Omicron, and to the outside world, they were military consultants, meeting with presidents and generals from every allied nation. In reality, they were dealers of death, willing to kill countless civilians for the right price. Justifying their actions by using the tainted money to fund missions and objectives that weren't exactly kosher. Approved by someone high up in the government. Someone who needed to be exposed if Omicron was to be stopped.

She'd had to leave the ledgers when she'd escaped from the country. It had been Nate's team who'd gotten them out. His Delta unit, the best of the best, had been hand-picked to go to Kosovo. They'd had one mission—to destroy a lab in Serbia where terrorists were making a chemical weapon. They would have done it, too, if she and Harper and Tam hadn't told them the truth. God, she'd never forget Nate's face when he realized his country had betrayed him. They'd gone to the lab on recon, and confirmed that it wasn't terrorists making the gas, it was scientists, mostly young, bright graduate students, all working separately on their own unique task, none aware that when all the pieces were put together, they would have created the deadliest chemical agent known to man. They also didn't know that once the project was complete, none of them would live to spend the money they'd earned, or to write up their findings in the scientific journals. They'd been duped, just like Nate's unit had been duped. All by the men behind Omicron. Almost six months later, she'd gotten in touch with Branislav. It had taken another six months till he'd agreed to get the copies.

Unfortunately, they were a mess. It was going to take Kate weeks to put them in order, then to create the paper trail that could be used in court. *If* the papers were all there. If Omicron, the CIA covert operation that was out to kill her, kill them all, didn't find her first.

The reminder got her moving. She stepped out of the car, then decided not to make any phone calls from the street. Even though her cell couldn't be traced, she knew enough about microphones that she didn't dare talk in public. Hell, after what had happened to Christie, she knew talking in private wasn't safe, either.

She thought about Christie, and how Omicron had tormented her. One of the agents had dated her, then stalked her for months. She'd lost her job, her money, almost her sanity. All because she was Nate Pratchett's sister. Nate, who'd been Kate's go-to guy in Kosovo, had been in hiding. Everyone, including his sister, including Kate, had thought he was dead. But he'd been spending his time finding out who was involved in the Kosovo killings.

She wished Nate were here now. Nate, Seth, Boone and Cade, her Delta Force soldiers, all were in hiding. Nate and Seth were in Los Angeles, Boone was in Wyoming with Christie, and Cade was in Colorado, living in a safe house where they could all hide if they had to and listening in on the operations of a small Omicron office outside of Colorado Springs.

Kate headed inside to the ugly efficiency apartment she'd rented under yet another assumed name. The smell of unwashed bodies and weed filled the dim hall, and for once, she didn't mind.

VINCE WAITED IN the manager's office, shifting on the too-small chair, willing himself to chill. The guy, name of Tyson, was prissy and nervous and Vince needed his help. It turned out he wasn't sure who had been assigned to stock Tim's bar, and he had to go find the paperwork.

The office gave him no easy distractions—it was as prim as the man who occupied it. The chairs were like something out of a Victorian sitting room, too delicate for a man Vince's size. The art was all landscapes, the lamps had little beads on the shades and the whole office smelled like his grandmother's bedroom.

He tried to regret smashing Baker in the face but couldn't. Then he tried to figure out which gang was most likely to have wanted Tim dead, but that just made him fidget more.

Finally, he stood. At least he wouldn't break the chair. He walked over to the window and looked out. It was gloomy, a typical November day for Los Angeles. At least there was no snow. He'd grown up in South Dakota, and he'd seen enough snow there to last two lifetimes.

He was on the third floor, and from this corner window he could see a couple of patrol cars. More interesting was the vendor, selling fish tacos and *horchata,* standing by the front entrance. He'd probably witnessed the gunmen enter the hotel, although he'd probably be too scared to be of any help.

"Detective Yarrow."

Vince turned. Tyson walked in with two manila folders.

"The woman taking care of the fourteenth floor is Kate Rydell. I've asked her supervisor to bring her here."

"Great." He nodded at the folders. "May I take a look?"

The man handed them over, and Vince turned slightly, giving the manager more of his back, hoping he'd catch the hint.

In the folder, he found Rydell's work application along with a very blurry copy of her driver's license. Shit, he couldn't get anything from the picture at all. It was even hard to make out the license number or the salient facts. Squinting, he saw that she was five-eight, one hundred eighteen pounds, and had brown hair and eyes. That wouldn't get him far. "I'll need copies," he said, not bothering to turn. He checked her license address against the application information. They were the same. Her work history was just about what he expected. Hotel service, waitress. High school education.

He heard the manager behind him and handed him the first folder. "Do you have surveillance cameras?"

"In the lobby and in the garage."

"I'll need them."

"Why don't you come with me. You can watch the tapes while I get the photocopies. We can wait for Ms. Rydell in the security office."

Luckily, the woman who was in charge of security for the hotel thought on her feet. She'd already taken out the tapes from this morning and queued them for duplication. Her name was Phyllis Samms, and from what he could see she was a regular on the weight machines. He'd hate to run into her in a dark alley.

Even her handshake was muscular. "I've got them ready," she said, pointing to a chair. He sat down. "I couldn't find your shooter in the lobby. Maybe your people will have more luck. However, there are some interesting shots in the garage."

She sat next to him and pressed the remote. The camera angle wasn't good—it was aimed more for identifying cars than people. Someone would have to look up in order for him to get a good face shot. Phyllis was right, there were some interesting shots. Two guys in big coats with hoods ran out at eleven-seventeen. He couldn't see who they were, not even tats, but he'd take the tape and let the lab boys go to town. They'd find something.

The bangers didn't get in a car. Instead they ran out of camera range.

As Phyllis went to stop the tape, Vince shook his head. He kept watching. A couple of businessmen came out, got into their cars. A hotel employee, a male, came out for a cigarette. Then nothing until a police car came in, followed by an ambulance.

He watched as his own unmarked car entered the garage. Jeff got out, then he did, and they walked right into the building.

Nothing except cops and EMTs and then, a woman. She was in a blue uniform and she had dark hair. Slim, tall—it had to be Kate Rydell.

She glanced at the official vehicles, then walked calmly to her car, a beat-up old Toyota Celica. Nothing about her was rushed or panicked. Still, she wasn't wearing a coat, which told him she hadn't stopped to clock out or to go to her locker. She got her keys out of her pocket and opened her door.

That's when he saw her face. It was nothing like the

picture on her driver's license. Even though the security
camera wasn't the best, he could see she was a very attractive woman. Her hair had been pulled back, so he got a
pretty decent look. She didn't seem like a room service
employee. Not with those cheekbones.

"You know her?" he asked Phyllis.

"Not really. I've seen her around, but we've never
talked."

"No?"

"She kept to herself. I've never seen her with anyone.
Expect maybe Ellen."

Vince got out his notebook. "Ellen?"

While Phyllis gave him the details about the housekeeper, he thought about Kate Rydell. She must have
known something about the gangbangers who'd killed
Tim. She'd gotten out so damn fast, he knew she was
running, that she didn't want anyone to know she'd seen
the whole thing. She wasn't about to cooperate, not willingly. But in the end, she would. He'd make sure of that.

2

THE MOTEL WAS AS nondescript as its name. The Sleep Inn had only twenty rooms, and the one she requested was on the second floor, on the end, with windows facing the parking lot and Van Nuys Boulevard. It cost thirty-nine dollars plus tax a night.

She put the cardboard box on the small round table and looked around the room. A double bed with an ugly green bedspread, a TV bolted to a squat dresser. A phone she wouldn't use. The carpet was worn and seemed recently vacuumed. The sink tile was cracked, but the water pressure wasn't bad. She'd stayed in worse places. Lots worse.

For the first time since she'd witnessed the murder, she let herself take a moment. In the past two hours she'd packed, loaded her car and gone by several other motels until she'd found this one. It was far enough from her old apartment that she felt relatively safe, but not so far she couldn't hook up with the others.

Seth and Nate were working on something big, tailing some high-level employee of Omicron—that was when they weren't trying to earn a living with their private security business. They'd both been surveillance experts in Kosovo. When they'd gotten back, they'd spent every last cent setting up a trauma room in Harper's basement. Just in case. Not only couldn't they get regular jobs any longer, they couldn't do half the things normal people took for granted. Go to a hospital, for example. At least not for the kinds of injuries they were likely to get fighting Omicron. Even she'd had to learn to shoot, and Kate had always hated guns.

Harper worked at the free clinic in Boyle Heights, but she was always on call in case anything happened to any member of the team. They hadn't had to use her services so far. She had been one of the doctors for the U.N. staff Kate had met in Kosovo. Harper had seen firsthand what Omicron had created in the Balkans. It had been her misfortune to be taken to the remote Serbian village that had been the testing ground for the gas. A nurses' aide hadn't been able to reach her family, so she'd asked Harper to drive with her to her home town. Everyone there was dead. Men, women, children. A town full of life, wiped out in one awful morning.

Then Kate had met Tamara, a chemist who thought she'd been working to eliminate biological and chemical weapons, but in truth Omicron had tricked her and a lot of other scientists into creating a chemical agent of unimaginable horror. Tam had rebelled, and now she was one of them. One of the six who were hunted.

But Kate hadn't talked to either of the women in a long time. She was too busy trying to earn a living and trying to make sense of the poor photocopies from Kosovo. Her days swam by in dread and tedium. The fear never left. Never. It had become her second heartbeat. Now this.

She didn't have enough horror in her life? She would have screamed her outrage if she thought it would do any good. That poor man in the hotel, to die such an ugly death. She wondered if he'd been married. If he had children.

She got her cell from her purse and dialed Nate's number. It rang twice.

"Yeah."

"I've got trouble."

"What?"

"It's not Omicron. But it's bad. I witnessed a murder today at the hotel."

"Shit. Where are you now?"

"At a motel in Reseda. I got out, left the apartment. No one followed."

"Okay, that's good."

"What's not good is that I saw them. Gangbangers. I can identify them."

"No, you can't."

"Yes, I can. I saw their faces. And the tattoos, and their weapons."

"Kate, you can't. The moment you come forward, you're dead. You know that, right?"

"There has to be a way. I can't just—"

"There is no way. I'm sorry. I know this sucks, but it's not just you. It's all of us. We're getting close. We can't afford to be identified. And you have to finish the paper trail."

She let her head drop down, so weary she could hardly breathe. "It's not fair."

"Damn straight it's not."

"Okay. Fine. I'll keep my mouth shut. There's another problem. I didn't get my last check. I'm really broke."

"Damn. We just had a major outlay of cash. Not much left in the coffers. Let me see what I can do."

"Okay."

"Can you make it a week?"

"If I have to."

"Sorry, kiddo. I mean it. I'll figure something out."

"I appreciate it. What about getting me a new name?"

"That, I can have for you by tomorrow. Give me a call in the morning."

"Okay. Thanks." She turned the phone off but didn't move. There were clothes to hang up, her files to go through. But first, that shower she'd been aching for. There'd been a time in her life when she'd adored showers and baths. She'd indulged in every kind of ointment and bath goody she could find. She'd had something for every mood.

Now she carried a good soap with her because her face got too dry if she used the cheap stuff. That was it. Good soap. No lotions, no salts, no special conditioning treatments. Most days it didn't matter. But man, today she'd kill for a lavender bubble bath.

NATE DISCONNECTED and dropped the cell phone on the makeshift table in front of him. He leaned back and closed his eyes, willing himself to relax. He tried to remember how long it had been since he'd had a really good night's sleep.

His eyes popped open, and, momentarily panicked, he looked at his watch. Fifteen minutes. He'd lost fifteen minutes.

He stumbled to his feet and took the ten steps to the bathroom. He turned on the cold water and splashed some on his face, then dried and looked at himself in the mirror.

He had to admit he was looking a little gaunt. Who was he kidding? He looked like crap. Would you buy a customized security system from this man?

He sighed and ran his fingers through his hair. Several times. He actually picked up the brush and made a moderate effort to look somewhat neat.

Kate. He had to find some way to help Kate.

As refreshed as he was likely to get at the moment, he went back into his living room. Well, there wasn't much he could cut back on. The only table in the room was a piece of plywood on concrete blocks. He'd gotten the mattress at Goodwill. His phone, like everybody else's in the team, was prepaid—virtually untraceable. He'd never turned on the gas, doing all his cooking on a camp stove—on his plywood table. The couch had come with the room.

Everything went into equipment and the needs of the team.

He picked up his cell and dialed Seth's. He knew the number by heart, just as he knew everyone else's. No little scraps of paper lying about to get found later.

"Hello?"

"Seth. It's Nate."

"Something new?"

"Kate's in trouble."

Nate could hear movement on the phone.

"Shit. Where is she? I could be there in…"

"Not that kind of trouble. She ran into a situation. She's got to relocate."

"A-a-ah. Okay. The usual? Driver's license, birth certificate…"

"Yeah. Pretty quick, too. And how are you fixed for cash?"

Seth let loose a strangled laugh. "I gave the last of it to you for that surveillance equipment. Maybe in a week."

Nate sighed. "Don't sweat it. Just get to work on her new ID, would you?"

"Sure thing. And Nate?"

"Yeah?"

"Get some sleep."

"WHAT THE FUCK were you thinking?"

Vince looked at Captain Emerson's red face, and he knew he wasn't gonna walk out of this smelling like a rose. "He accused Tim of being in bed with drug dealers."

"So what?"

"It wasn't true."

"Since when is that something new? He's not just putting the assault in the paper, he's putting it on Channel 5."

"How much does he want?"

"He says he wants twenty-million. What he really wants is your badge."

Vince sat back in the wooden chair across from Emerson's desk. He'd been in here a lot during his years on the force. Mostly to get chewed out. He didn't blame the Captain for that. He had a department to run. He had people to answer to. The Captain understood, most of the time. He knew Vince did the job.

Most cops who got involved with investigating gangs didn't last a year. They'd transfer to anything else they could, knowing it was the most dangerous of all the details. Hell, he knew guys who would quit rather than do one day on the streets. And Vince had stuck with it for three years already. "You gonna give it to him?"

The Captain, looking a lot older today than he had yesterday, wiped his face with the flat of his hand. "I gotta suspend you. You know that, right? I can't just give you a slap on the wrist this time. Goddammit, Vince. You had to hit him in the face?"

"Yeah, Captain. I did."

"Shit, I suppose so. I'll do what I can to soothe some feathers, but it's not gonna be quick. Maybe the time off will do you good."

Vince leaned forward. "They killed Tim. I'm not gonna let that go."

"You have no choice."

He opened his mouth, then shut it before he got in deeper. Instead, he got out his badge and his weapon and put them on the desk. "Call me when I can come back."

The Captain looked at him for a long moment. "Don't do anything stupid. Well, stupider. This may not be up to me. You got it?"

Vince nodded as he stood, grateful it was only a suspension. "Thanks."

"Idiot."

"Nothing new there."

The Captain let him go. "Get out of town. Go get drunk. Get laid. Relax."

"I'll do my best."

Emerson was already on the phone when Vince got to the door. The Captain had the press to deal with, and the city council and the mayor. It was all part of a thankless job, and keeping Vince's badge was way, way down there in terms of importance. But that didn't change things.

There was no way in hell he was going to let this thing go. He had Kate Rydell's address in his pocket. He'd find her, question her about what she saw, get her to testify if necessary. If it got him fired, oh, well. It was time for him to leave the job, anyway. He didn't have the heart for it anymore.

He walked into the squad room and to his desk. He unlocked the bottom drawer and reached far into the back, where he pulled out a black leather case. He didn't open it until he was outside.

Once he got in his car, he took out a badge. He wasn't supposed to have it, let alone use it. But it went into his pocket, and the gun under his seat went into his holster. Screw it.

THE KOSOVO PAPERS on her desk beckoned, but the want ads were more important, at least for the moment. She had two sections, one for jobs and one for furnished apartments. With red pen in hand, she started with the jobs.

The primary criterion was the invisibility factor. Room service had been great for that. She'd also been a waitress, a housekeeper and worked at a copy store. Since she'd returned from Kosovo, the one time she'd tried to do anything close to her qualifications, she'd been forced to quit, leaving the R & D company in a real bind. She wouldn't do that again.

It had only been a few months since she'd seen the depths to which Omicron would go to stop her and her friends. They'd terrorized Christie, an innocent woman whose only crime was being Nate's sister. It had come to a bloody end, and if things hadn't worked out, they could have all been killed.

Despite everything she'd seen, it was still hard for her to grasp that it was the U.S. government after them. The public didn't know about this side of their government, and wouldn't, unless she and the others could put together enough hard evidence to prove what they knew beyond doubt was true.

If it had just been Omicron, it would have been easier, but someone—someone very powerful—was making sure the group was funded. It wasn't enough to lay out the paper trail of deceit and murder. Kate and her friends had to dig deep into the black heart of the organization and find out who was pulling the strings.

One thing at a time. She had to get a job. She needed a place to live. But first, she needed her new name, a new ID, a new license plate for her car.

Nate was handling that. Right now she had to find the job and the apartment. And she had to figure out how to do it damn fast, because her money situation was more dire than she'd imagined.

If only she could use her savings. She had over sixty-thousand dollars in a bank account in Washington, D.C., but she couldn't touch it. Well, maybe she didn't have it anymore—now that her family thought she was dead.

So, she had seventy-four dollars to her name. That was it. And one night in this motel was going to eat up half of that. How was she going to get an apartment with no security or first month's rent? Which meant she was probably going to end up sleeping in her car for a while.

She felt vulnerable enough behind locked doors, but to be on the street? In a rusty old heap of a car? She thought about asking Nate or Harper to take her in, but that could put them in danger, what with the police likely searching for her. There had to be a way to get her check from the hotel. She didn't want any favors, just what she was owed.

She put her pen down and picked up her cell. There was no way she could go get the check herself. Perhaps there was something she could do.

She had Ellen's number listed in her phone. Kate had taken the housekeeper to work a few times when her husband hadn't come home in time for her to get the car. It was six-forty, so the shift was over. It would be safe now to call.

The phone rang so many times that Kate almost hung up, but finally an out-of-breath Ellen answered.

"I'm interrupting," Kate said.

"No, I was just doing laundry, and I couldn't get to the phone. Kate?"

"Yeah."

"Where did you go? I heard you were up in that guy's room when he was shot."

"No. I wasn't. I was down the hall."

"Oh. The cops think you were there."

"They're wrong. I was close enough though to hear the gunfire."

"Is that why you left like that, in the middle of a shift?"

"Yep. I was scared. I'm sorry to do that to Mr. Tyson, but I couldn't help it."

"You should probably call and tell them you didn't see anything."

"I will. I promise." Kate squeezed her eyes shut and crossed her fingers. "Uh, could you do me a favor?"

"If I can."

"Could you pick up my check for me tomorrow? We could meet for coffee after work. At the Copper Skillet."

"Oh, sure. No sweat. You'll have to be there right at six because I have to get the car back to Rick."

"Absolutely. I'll be there before six. Thanks, Ell. You're a doll."

"It's nothing. Just don't forget to tell the boss, you know? And the cops."

"Right. I'll do that. Thanks."

"Sure. See you tomorrow."

Kate disconnected the phone and closed her eyes, though this time it was with relief. Two weeks pay would get her into an apartment. It was going to be in a lousy part of town, but it beat sleeping in the car. She blessed Ellen in all kinds of ways, mostly for just being nice.

The warm fuzzy feeling lasted about ten seconds, then she turned back to the ads. If she got a job first, she'd know where to find the apartment. No reason she couldn't get an interview tomorrow afternoon. If Nate came through with her new identity.

She circled every menial job she could find, from the San Fernando Valley to Torrance. With that done and the promise of cash tomorrow, she went to get some dinner. There was a place she knew where they sold burritos, big ones, for a couple of bucks. That would do.

THE APARTMENT WAS completely empty. Not a matchbook, a hairpin or a paper cup. Kate Rydell traveled light and fast. What was she running from? An abusive husband? A criminal warrant? Whatever it was, her behavior told Vince she wasn't going to answer questions willingly. He'd have to find out more about her so that he could apply pressure. He didn't give a damn about her reasons, she was going to help him put Tim's killers behind bars. How hard it was going to be was up to her.

He turned to the super who'd let him in. "She was here last night?"

"I told ya. She was here this morning, too."

"You didn't see her leave?"

The man shook his head, which made his jowls quiver. "No. I musta been showing an apartment."

"She didn't leave a forwarding address? A note? A number?"

"Nah, nothing. Too bad. She always paid in cash, on time, and she never made any trouble."

Vince thanked the man, and as he went back to his car he realized the only option he had left was to find Kate's friend Ellen. No way in hell he was letting his only witness get away.

KATE SAT IN THE LAST booth against the back wall at the Copper Skillet. She kept her eyes on the door, even though it would be at least five more minutes before Ellen could conceivably get there.

The day had been long and tense. Nate had arranged a new identity for her, but he couldn't get his hands on the paperwork until tomorrow morning. Her new name would be Kate Hogan. She was glad he'd remembered to use Kate again. She'd used it now for four different identities. It was simply too difficult for her to change her first name over and over. She needed to react quickly, seamlessly, and always being a Kate helped.

She had to get through tonight, then go to Gino's tomorrow to pick up her new ID. She'd only been to the pizza parlor once. It wasn't only a pizzeria. It was also an emergency meeting place. The phone there was always monitored, via a nifty computer program Seth had written, and Gino, an ex-Delta Force sharpshooter, had given them a safe place to hide. There, she'd change the license plates on her car, then she'd start in on the interviews. That part wouldn't be too bad. Nate, bless his heart, had provided references for Kate Hogan, and she had several places lined up. Of course, she couldn't do much of anything until she cashed her check.

It was almost six, and she sipped her coffee, watching every person who walked into the restaurant. Four minutes later, she sighed with relief when Ellen entered, still wearing her uniform. Ellen had a rough life, especially with her four kids to feed. Her husband was an undocumented worker in the garment district, and they had to pay for childcare, as well as all the other expenses. Kate had no idea how they got by.

"Hey," Ellen said as she slipped into the booth. "You didn't call Tyson."

"I know. I will."

"The cops came to see me."

Kate's heart froze. "What did you tell them?"

"Nothing. Except that you didn't see the murder."

"Did you tell them you were meeting me here?"

"Hell, no. I don't tell cops my business. I figured you'd call them when you were ready, but jeez, Kate. Give me a break. I don't need that."

"I know. You're right. I'll have it straightened out by tomorrow. I promise."

"You better. Shit, can you imagine if they come to the house?"

"No, no, they won't. I'll call. They won't bother you again."

Ellen pushed her brittle blond hair behind her ears, then she opened her purse. It was all Kate could do not to snatch the pay envelope from her hand. "Mr. Tyson was pissed you quit without telling him. I said it was a personal thing."

"What did he say?"

Ellen smiled. "That you were ungrateful and downright rude."

Kate grinned. That was Mr. Tyson all right.

"I have to go or Ricky's gonna kill me. He's got a job tonight."

"Okay, thanks, Ellen. You have no idea how much this helped."

"Hey, we're friends, right? Let me know when this whole cop thing is over with, huh?"

"You bet," Kate said, knowing it was a lie. She hated so much about her life now, but this… This was hell. She'd never betrayed a friend before Kosovo. Not ever. And now, it was becoming second nature.

VINCE WATCHED ELLEN leave the parking lot, and his gaze turned back to the Copper Skillet entrance. He knew Kate was inside, but he wasn't going to approach her in such a public place.

He sipped his cold coffee, waiting. He was good at that. God knew he'd had enough practice. The longer he sat, the more he thought about Tim and the pricks who'd killed him.

He'd gone to see Tim's wife that afternoon, and for a man who'd been involved with death for more years than he cared to remember, it had ripped his heart out to see her, weeping like a child at the loss of her husband. Vince had tried to find the right words, but Tim's death was so wrong there was nothing at all that he could say. Except that he wouldn't rest until justice was served.

There she was. Kate Rydell, walking out of the restaurant, her head low, almost hidden in her big coat. When she got to her car, she looked in the back seat, then all around her before she slipped the key in the door.

He waited until she drove past him to start his pursuit. This was something else he was good at. Following without being seen.

She drove carefully, never over the speed limit. All surface streets, with a hell of a lot of turns. Finally, she got to a dive motel in Reseda, and he waited and watched as she walked up the stairs to the far unit on the second floor.

It was showtime.

3

KATE'S HAND SHOOK AS she took the check out of her purse once again, praying she'd misread the amount. But no, it was half of what it should have been, not even three hundred dollars. She wanted to call Tyson and scream at him, but she couldn't, could she? The deductions, of course. For the uniform she'd not returned, for her locker—which were in addition to tax deductions.

Altogether, more had been taken out than paid, putting her in an incredible bind. She'd never get an apartment and money for gas, food or much else, with this. Until Nate could come up with more cash, she was stuck here. In this dingy room, with the noise from the street keeping her up at night.

It wasn't fair, but that had become the central theme of her life: Not Fair. Should Have Been Different. If Only.

She sat on the edge of the bed, the springs squeaking as if she weighed a ton. At least she had enough money to get to her interviews. It would have to do.

It took all her will, but she got up, put her coat in the measly closet and figured she'd make herself some tea, then start work on the ledgers. The tea, one of the essentials in her life along with her good soap, daily showers and a warm bed, would be made with her little heat coil. She'd picked it up in a travel shop four years ago and had taken it everywhere. She could survive on packaged soup, instant oatmeal and tea if she had to. Just add water.

From the closet floor, she got her box with the ledger pages and her laptop and put it next to the small table. But before she could get her cup, there was a knock on the door. Panic made her freeze and foolishness made her hope it was a mistake.

"Kate Rydell? It's the police. Open up, please."

Shit, shit, shit. Should she keep quiet and hope the cops hadn't seen her come in? How in hell had they found her? Ellen. It had to be Ellen. Kate cursed again, knowing her friend hadn't purposely betrayed her.

"I know you're in there. Open the door."

Kate shoved the box under the table, then went to obey. "Please hold your badge up to the peephole."

He did, and she memorized the number, knowing all the while Omicron wouldn't have a bit of trouble getting a fake badge. Or hiring a cop to do their dirty work.

"Open the door, Kate."

She bristled at the use of her first name, but she managed not to shake as she turned the deadbolt. "Yes?"

The man on the other side looked as if he'd had a rough day. He was taller than her by a good five inches, wearing a brown overcoat. His tie was loosened and he hadn't shaved in a day or two. His dark hair was messy, as if he'd run his hands through it and not looked in a mirror after. It was his eyes that really gave him away. They were oddly blue and filled with anger. "I'm here about the murder at the hotel."

She thought about telling him he had the wrong person but dismissed that approach immediately. "What do you want to know?"

He looked past her into her room. "May I come in?"

"I don't suppose it would do me any good to say no."

"We could always do this at the precinct."

She opened the door. Only after he was inside did it occur to her that he was alone. Her eyes narrowed. "Where's your partner?"

"He'll be here shortly. I'm Detective Yarrow, and I know you witnessed Tim Purchase's murder."

"And how do you know that?"

"Your cart was there. Open. And you hadn't even finished restocking the refrigerator. I also have you on tape ten minutes after the murder, leaving the hotel."

"I was there, but I didn't see anything."

"You were behind the bar."

"That's right. Where I hid."

"You could see everything from there. In the mirror."

"I suppose that would be true," she said, "if I'd been looking up. I wasn't."

"You mean to tell me you didn't see any part of it? Not even when he opened the door?"

"That's what I'm telling you."

"But you heard it."

"Gunfire. That's all. I'm sorry. I wish I could help, but I can't."

The anger in his eyes had turned to fury. His neck had darkened and his hands were fisted by his side. She'd faced a lot of angry men in her life and she knew this cop would stop at nothing. "You're lying."

"Excuse me?"

He stepped closer to her. "If you didn't see anything, why did you run?"

"Gunshots. A dead guy."

"A dead *guy?* Do you have any idea who it was lying up there in a pool of blood?"

"No."

He turned briefly, running his hand through that tangle of hair. When he turned back, he seemed the tiniest bit calmer. "He was important. He was also a friend."

"As I said, I wish I could help. But I can't."

"I can protect you."

She laughed. She shouldn't have, because he was so very serious. And because it told him more than she wanted him to know.

He almost smiled at her slip. "Did you recognize the gang? Were they wearing colors? Tattoos?"

"I didn't see them."

"Don't. I just want to know—"

"Detective Yarrow, I appreciate that you're trying to find whoever killed this man, but you'd be wise to look elsewhere. I can't help you."

"You can. And you will."

She closed her eyes for a moment, and when she opened them again, he was studying her so closely she had to step away. "You're mistaken."

"No, I'm not. Listen to me, Kate. I need these punks. I need them like you wouldn't believe. I'm willing to do whatever it takes to get them." He took a step closer, bridging the gap. "Whatever it takes."

"I applaud your determination," she said, standing her ground. "You're asking for something I can't give."

He didn't say anything as he continued to stare.

Those strange blue eyes looked deeply, and she touched her throat. Then he broke away and walked over to the small table.

The hairs on the back of her neck stood up. She was terrified that he'd look in the box underneath, that somehow he would understand what she had in her possession. The toe of his brown shoe touched the side of the box, and he turned his head so he could see.

Kate wanted to stop him, but she knew if she responded at all it would just increase his curiosity. The best thing she could do was act nonchalant. As if his questions weren't making her feel guilty as hell, as if her very life and the lives of her friends didn't depend on her lies.

If only her heart wouldn't beat so hard. She felt sure he could hear it, that if he stayed one more minute he'd uncover the truth.

"Listen up, Kate," he said, his voice very low, a whisper that made everything worse. "I know you saw who killed my friend. I know you ran because you think the gangs will come after you if you testify. Well, here's the deal. I don't care. I don't like being lied to, and believe me, I've been lied to by the best, so you don't fool me for a second."

"I think you should leave," she said, but this time her bravado slipped and her voice quavered like a child's.

"I'm not leaving until I get what I want. I'm going to be on you twenty-four-seven. And to make things even more interesting, I'm going to let the press know what I'm doing. You hear me? If you think you're afraid now, just wait."

Vince watched her face grow pale, her eyes widen

with his threats. She'd seen everything, all right. He'd wager his life on it. And he wasn't about to let her walk away without testifying.

"That's illegal. It's harassment."

"Sue me."

"Don't you even care that you'll be wasting your time on me when you could be looking for the killers?"

"We've got a whole department of cops doing just that. My only assignment is you."

She turned from him and walked over to the bed, but she didn't sit. He knew she was trying to figure a way out of this, to make him leave. Not that she had a prayer.

He relaxed, debated taking off his coat, but didn't. Instead he studied her.

The cameras in the garage hadn't done her justice. She was a beautiful woman, classy, strong. Her long, dark hair was shiny and as smooth as her skin. She wore no makeup, at least as far as he could tell, but it didn't make a difference. With those dark eyes, that long, lean body, she could have had any man in the blink of an eye. So why didn't she? She carried herself like someone with money. It didn't track that she was working for room service.

Clearly, she was hiding. From what, he didn't know, but he'd find out.

She moved again, lifting her head, straightening her shoulders. "I would help you if I could, but I can't. If you let the press know about me, I'll be as dead as your friend, whether the killers think I can ID them or not."

He held himself still, not wanting to spook her. "Why?"

"Someone's after me. A stalker."

"Let me help."

She frowned. "Yeah, right. And your success rate in finding and convicting stalkers is what?"

"Pretty damn good."

"Now, who's lying?"

"Just tell me what I want to know, then you can play hide-and-seek all you want."

She sighed and sat on the edge of the bed. "I have nothing to tell you. Nothing, you hear me? I hid. I heard gunshots. Running. By the time I looked up, your friend was dead and I was alone with him in the room. Okay? There isn't anything more."

Vince shook his head. "Sorry. It was a good try, but I'm not buying it."

"Buying what?"

"You know more than you're telling me."

"What are you talking about?"

"You know how long I've been doing this? You know how many people have lied to me?"

"This time you're wrong."

He looked at her. Through her. "I've been wrong about a lot of things. But not this. Seriously. I have nothing else on the docket. Just you, until you tell me the truth."

"If you enjoy wasting your time, be my guest. But you can't do it sitting in my room." She walked over to the door and opened it, her lips tight, her posture more closed off now than when he'd first arrived.

"You bet. I'll leave, but I won't be far. You can count on that. No matter where you go, there I'll be."

She said nothing. She didn't even watch him as he passed her. Her gaze was somewhere else, perhaps with the stalker she said was after her, perhaps on the vision of Tim on the bloody carpet. It didn't matter. Not a bit.

The second he'd cleared the door, it was closed, not slammed, behind him. He got out his cell phone as he headed for his car.

Surveillance wasn't terribly effective without sufficient manpower. He wasn't fool enough to believe he could cover her without getting sloppy. He dialed Jeff.

"Detective Stoller."

"Hey, I've got an interesting challenge for you, buddy."

Jeff's groan was all too familiar. Vince didn't pay any attention to it as he detailed what he needed Jeff to do. Kate Rydell was now a material witness. Since Vince was on suspension, Jeff would have to do the paperwork and get the manpower.

In the meantime, Vince would get comfortable in his car. He wasn't sure when Kate would make her move, only that she would attempt to flee.

He was also going to look into her background. He'd soon find out if there was any truth to the stalker business or if Ms. Rydell was hiding something even worse.

ALTHOUGH THEY ADVERTISED Never Empty, Never Closed, there were few customers at The Pantry coffee shop. Nate scanned the tables, his gaze finally settling on an occupied booth near the far window. He walked across the diner and sat down across from his old friend. "Seth," he said. "Good to see you."

"Good to see you, brother." The two men ordered coffee when the elderly waitress asked if they wanted some and spread the menus in front of them.

"I almost didn't recognize you with the glasses," Nate said.

Seth shrugged off his stained leather jacket, revealing a plain black T-shirt. "Good. Let's hope no one else does."

Nate smiled wryly. They seldom saw each other, wisely keeping their distance in case one of them went down. "You have everything, I trust."

Seth nodded, his gaze on the menu. "I have about eight bucks. What about you?"

"Enough for a decent breakfast. Let's splurge." There'd been a time when Nate had never had to think about money. He'd always had plenty to spend on women and booze. Not from his work in Delta Force, but from a little locking device he'd come up with just after college. It didn't look like much, but he'd sold the Army on the usefulness of the lock on weaponry in the field, and they'd bought the patent. The money was to be his nest egg, his safety net in case he got hurt. But it was all gone now. He'd spent a bloody fortune on Harper's basement trauma room and Tam's lab and equipment.

The waitress came back and they both ordered the bacon and egg breakfast. When they were alone again, Seth pulled an envelope from the inside pocket of his jacket and wordlessly handed it across the table.

Nate glanced around, then flipped through the contents. Driver's license, Social Security card, birth certificate. He held the driver's license where the streetlight shone on it. "Damn. Your guy does fine work."

"Computer nerd at Cal Tech. He did these, too." He put two photo IDs on the table.

Nate stuffed Kate's documents back in the envelope and picked up one of the identification cards. "Midtown Electric," he read. "Damn. Where'd you get this picture?"

"Department of Defense," Seth said.

"I must've been in high school." He peered closer. "Frank Foley?"

"George Hale." Seth pushed the glasses all the way up the bridge of his nose. "Pleased to meet you." He clipped the ID on the neck of his T-shirt.

The waitress arrived with their food, and Nate quickly secured Kate's documents and then clipped his ID onto his flannel shirt. After dinner, they'd do one more recon on one of the offices of Omicron. While it looked like a normal building, filled with consultants and secretaries, Nate had learned that it was actually an operations center for the rogue CIA unit. Most of their operatives had either been fired from the CIA or were professional mercenaries. They worked in secret, and while Nate had discovered several maneuvers that would never have been sanctioned by congress, including two high level assassinations, all he really cared about now was the chemical weapon they'd engineered in Kosovo.

The gas had striking similarities to VX, but with VX there were antidotes. Nothing stopped this new weapon from killing. Death was ugly—the chemical bound itself to the enzyme that transmits signals to the nerves and inhibits them, making them uncontrollable. In the liquid form, the chemical takes an hour to kill, in the gaseous state, minutes.

The truly horrifying thing about it was that Nate knew there was a market for this thing. The Sudan. Nicaragua. Not to mention the Middle East. And that was just off the top of his head. There was money to be made in certain death, and the men behind Omicron had no qualms about raking it in. There was no choice in

Nate's mind. They had to be stopped before even one shipment of the gas was sold.

Halfway through the large breakfast, Seth laid his fork along the side of the plate, took a sip of the coffee and winced. "So how sure are you about this Leland Ingram?"

"Damned sure. I've been following him since before my return from the dead. His official title is Project Manager, but I have a feeling he's more like Omicron's chief henchman. If we can get inside and pull this off, we should be able to monitor everything they're doing. We can find out the status of the gas, but, more importantly, we can scope out exactly who's funding the operation, the man from Washington giving Omicron the go-ahead. There's no way for us to ever get these bastards unless we know who we're up against. This surveillance should be a big step forward."

Seth glanced at his watch. "We'd better finish up and get going."

Nate nodded, and the two men returned to their food. Minutes later, his plate clean, Seth laid down his fork, drank a little more coffee, and motioned to the waitress.

"You want more coffee?" she asked. Both men shook their heads, and she finished with the check and put it face down between them.

Seth slipped his jacket on, looking once again like another anonymous worker, and stood, picking up the check. He headed for the cashier as Nate donned his own jacket and fished a five out of his pocket. He met Seth outside the front door.

"Go home and get some sleep," Nate said. "I'll scope out the security on the building and we'll connect at Gino's."

Seth stretched his neck around and nodded. He, like the rest of the team, wore the stress of their work on his face. "You sure?" he asked. "Another fifteen minutes won't kill me."

Nate shook his head. "Nah. One of us should be alert at Gino's."

SHE DIDN'T SEE the detective when she left the motel at nine-thirty the next morning, but she was certain he was around somewhere. She'd talked to Nate last night, and he had everything she'd need to start the next life. They would move on the assumption that the police would be watching, so Kate would fill out a job application as a cover. Nate and Seth were going to be doing a little surveillance of their own, and get whatever information on Detective Yarrow they could, primarily to determine if he was on the level.

The most important thing for her was to pick up her new papers. She wasn't sure how she was going to ditch Yarrow, but she had to have the new ID.

Gino was one of the only people outside their group who understood what had happened in Kosovo, and he'd offered his place as a quasi-command post. All phone calls were taped, and if someone needed help, they'd dial the pizza parlor.

Kate fought another yawn as she battled the traffic on the freeway. Her night had been horrible. Not only had she gotten no work done, she'd gotten virtually no sleep.

She hated lying about not seeing the gangbangers. It went against everything she'd ever stood for. Not just the lying but not stepping forward, not taking a stand for what was right and just. But how could she when doing so would sign the death warrants of the people who had done so much that was right and just? If it had just been her own life...

She'd like to think she'd step forward. That she wouldn't let herself be intimidated and cowed by punks, even if they were killers.

The night had been filled with struggles. Trying to sleep in the unfamiliar bed. Searching desperately for a way out of her dilemma, and thinking about Detective Yarrow.

The truth was, she respected him, if not his tactics. He believed in what he was doing. His friend had been killed, and he wasn't going to let anything stand in the way of getting the men who'd done it. Yet he was the worst possible thing that could have happened to her.

She'd stopped asking why she'd been in that suite, at that moment. It was no use questioning fate. How could she have ever guessed that becoming a forensic accountant would lead her into a world of chemical warfare, covert operations and being completely cut off from everyone she'd ever known or loved? Who would have imagined getting caught up in a murder and gang warfare while restocking minibar fridges?

She kept checking the rearview mirror, but she hadn't had enough spy training. Yarrow could have been two cars behind and she wouldn't have known it.

Best to just get to Gino's and let Nate and Seth take over. Maybe they could figure out a way she could stay hidden and still help Yarrow get his killers.

Her mind went back to him again. Mostly his eyes. They were such an interesting color. Not powdery or like clouds… More like blue flame. Or maybe that was just his anger.

Despite his dishevelment, he was a good-looking man. With no wedding ring. That didn't mean he wasn't married. If he wasn't, he surely had a woman, or women. Men like him were chick magnets. Powerful, dangerous, commanding. Oh, yeah, he'd have them, all right. But not for keeps.

She knew his type only too well. Nate, she supposed, was her first exposure to hero wannabees. They'd gone out on a couple of dates when she'd first arrived in Kosovo. He'd been charming and funny, but he wasn't interested in anything close to a relationship. Not Nate. She'd never have guessed what a true hero he would turn out to be. Shane, on the other hand, was, to quote a phrase, all hat and no cowboy. He'd also been a soldier, but not in the special forces. He'd talked about how tough he was, how he led his men with an iron fist. But he'd really been nothing more than a bully. She'd dumped him as soon as she'd seen his true colors.

She wondered if Yarrow was like Nate or like Shane. It didn't matter. She wasn't going to get to know him at all, nor would she want to. It was far too risky to let anyone in, for any reason. At least now, with Yarrow tailing her, he'd leave Ellen alone.

Her exit was coming up, so she got into the right lane, wondering who she would be this time. There was so much that went into changing identities. She'd have to learn a whole history, put it on like a coat and wear it all the time. She wasn't sure how they managed it, but anyone looking into Kate Rydell's background would find nothing suspicious. She had a good but unremarkable work history, and had paid her income taxes. No huge debts, no property of her own. A wholly unremarkable person.

Now she would become another unremarkable person, looking for another invisible job. She'd probably have to switch cars altogether because Yarrow knew this one. She'd slip away. Again. Only this time, no friends. She'd been foolish to get to know Ellen even a little. It could have gotten her killed.

There was one other car in Gino's parking lot. She pulled in next to it, making sure she had plenty of escape room, and brought her big tote with her into the store. Of course, no one was there this early, just Gino. And Nate and Seth, but she wouldn't actually see them. At least not in the front of the store. Probably in the bathroom, if she knew anything about her soldiers.

Once inside, things moved along smoothly. She filled out an application and Gino, all six foot six of him, slipped a packet inside her tote so adeptly that no one could have seen. Then she gave him back the application, he shook her hand and she went to the ladies' room.

Nate was perched on the counter, Seth was crouched under the air dryer. They were in jeans and T-shirts, looking buff but not particularly dangerous. A very nice illusion.

"Did you see him?" she asked, getting right down to business.

Nate, looking better than he had the last time she saw him, nodded. "He's in a blue Crown Victoria. There's a Dodgers' bumper sticker on the back left."

She leaned against the wall, so weary she thought she could curl up and sleep on the floor. "I think he's legit," she said. "His friend was murdered. I saw it. He's not going to let it go."

"We'll get you out. We just need you to stay with it for another day or two, okay? We're working on a place for you."

"The car will be clean," Seth said as he stood up. "You just walk away from this one when we get you."

She nodded. "I know I have to go. But isn't there some way? Something I can do? Maybe leave a document? A testament to what I saw?"

"It wouldn't be admissible," Nate said.

"Maybe that doesn't matter."

Seth came over to her and put his hand on her shoulder. She closed her eyes, wishing for once that they were closer. Funny, they'd almost died together, done unbelievably hard things as a team, but hugging, that crossed the line.

"I'd better get out there," she said, patting his hand before she stepped away. "You have my money?"

Nate jumped down, and she thought again about how much he'd aged since… It must have been so hard on him, pretending to be dead for so long. He traded cash for her check, endorsed, of course. "We'll try and figure something out, okay?" he said. "In the meantime, be careful."

"Always." She left the bathroom, new ID and money safely tucked in her tote. She smiled at Gino as she walked into the cold November air.

Vince Yarrow was leaning on her car.

HE WISHED SHE WASN'T wearing the big coat. He wanted to see her in motion. She was a striking woman, and it wouldn't have bothered him at all to have met her under different circumstances.

He'd heard from Jeff about thirty minutes ago. The surveillance team was in place, although the Captain had only okayed six people. Eight would have been better. The first team would already be at the motel. He wasn't sure where Kate was going after this, but, wherever it was, he wouldn't be far behind.

"Did you get the job?" he asked pleasantly.

"Please get away from my car. I have appointments."

He pushed off the Toyota and smiled brightly, just to piss her off. "Great. Where are we going next?"

She looked daggers at him as she went around the front of the car.

"There's a simple way to get me to go."

Nothing. Not a look, not a glance.

"Maybe during the next interview, I'll come in. Who knows, they might want a character reference."

That got her. She spun on him, eyes narrow, lips tight. "I'm not one of the bad guys," she said. "I didn't hurt anyone. I didn't see anything. You're trying to get blood from stone."

He opened his mouth to argue, but a flash out of the corner of his eye made him turn. Behind a large trash bin was a familiar face. The bruise was new and rather spectacular.

"Wow," Vince said. "That looks like it's gotta hurt."

The reporter approached them, his camera in one hand, a small recorder in the other. "So this is your material witness?"

Vince blocked him with his body before he could reach Kate. "What the hell are you talking about?"

"I figured Emerson would like to know what you're up to."

"Emerson told me to relax. Get laid. I'm just following his advice."

"Bullshit, Yarrow. I know who she is."

"You don't know—" Vince stopped at the sound of the engine, and turned just in time to see Kate take off like a bat out of hell. Damn it.

"Oh, I like her," Baker said. "Feisty."

"Shut up, you asshole."

"See you in the funny papers." The reporter walked away, whistling, just to be a jerk.

Vince jogged to his car, cursing the reporter and cursing Kate. He had no idea where she'd gone, but he had to find her. If the gangbangers saw her picture in the paper, they'd make sure she'd never testify.

4

SHE CAME BACK AT SEVEN. Vince was sitting on the floor next to her motel door, a cold cup of coffee in his hand, a smile hiding his frustration at a day that had knocked the wind out of him. His informant Eddie, a junkie too long without a fix, had given him nothing at all, and it was only a matter of time until the Captain had his ass in a permanent sling.

"How's it going?" he asked.

Kate didn't look like her day had been much better. She stood in front of him, scowling. On her, it looked pretty good. "Nothing's changed. You're still making my life miserable. Who was that guy, and why did he take my picture?"

Vince got to his feet, his knees cracking like split kindling. "I've missed you. Any luck on the new job?"

"I'm not interested in chatting with you. I want you gone. Out of my life."

"No can do. Especially now."

She closed her eyes. "Why?"

"Well, I hate to be the bearer of bad tidings, but that wasn't a guy. It was a reporter."

She cursed, and, oddly, that looked good on her, too. "What have you done to me?"

"Me? I didn't do a thing. The minute you give me your statement, I'm all about protection. You wouldn't have a thing to worry about."

"Except for gangbangers coming to kill me."

"We should talk about that."

She gazed at him for a long moment. He needed a shower, a shave, some sleep. She wished he didn't.

Then she opened her door and walked silently into the motel room, leaving him to follow. She put her coat and bag away, ran a hand through that silky hair, then nodded toward the little table. "I've got tea and instant coffee."

"Coffee would be great."

"I hope you take it black."

"Yep." He took a wobbly seat and watched her move about the small, tidy room. Her clothes matched what he knew about her, that she'd gone from one low-level job to another, from one crummy apartment to the next. He still didn't quite believe the stalker story. Not because it couldn't have happened—that kind of crap was more prevalent than anyone wanted to believe—but because he'd found nothing about it in the records. No restraining orders, no complaints at all.

More than her plain sweater and beige pants, the thing that didn't fit her was her presence. She was a woman to be reckoned with. Nothing about her was timid or weak. He wanted, more than he should, to figure out this mystery.

She brought out a heating coil and plugged it in the wall, then took two foam cups and put in instant coffee for him, a tea bag for her. The whole process took about five minutes. He continued to watch. Mostly her hands, which were strong and lean, her nails short but neat, and her face, which showed no expression other than a quiet determination.

When she handed him the coffee, she took her tea and sat on the edge of the bed. "So talk."

Damn, he liked her. Straightforward, no games, not in the least coy. Other than lying through her teeth, she was all right. "The reporter's name is Baker, and he's a prick of the first order. I don't know how he found out about you. Maybe the same way I did."

"The videotape."

"Right."

"What paper does he work for?"

"The *Times*."

She looked away for a moment. When she looked back, she seemed infinitely tired. "Is there any way you can stop him from running the picture?"

"No."

"So these murderers are going to think I can ID them."

"Yes."

"And they'll come after me."

"Yes."

"Wonderful. Would it do any good for you to tell this reporter that I didn't see them?"

"I doubt it, but I can try."

She sipped her tea. "Are you telling me the truth? That you didn't tell Baker to force me into testifying?"

"I am. Although I still want you to do that."

"Why is it so hard for you to believe me?"

He put his cup down and leaned forward, his elbows on his knees. "I'd like to. Honest. But I was there. I crouched down, just where you'd have been, and I looked in that mirror. There's no way you would have known it was killers coming into the room. Tim heard a knock. He went to the door. You could see the door. It's human nature to look. You'd want to know. It's as simple as that."

"I was doing my job."

"Doesn't matter. You'd have looked. Anyone would have. And even if you saw them for a few seconds, that would have been enough. You would have seen if they were black, Caucasian, Hispanic, Asian. You'd have seen clothing. Weapons. Maybe tattoos."

"It makes a lot of sense, what you just said. But I didn't see. I would tell you if I did. I didn't."

He sat back up. "Sorry. Not buying it."

"When I was a kid," she said, "I had this phobia. I had nightmares about it, even though I have no recollection of where the fear started. I used to dream that I was being held prisoner and that I was being tortured. The guard wanted me to tell him something, but I had no clue what he was talking about. I wanted, more than anything, to tell him what he wanted to know, but I couldn't. So I just kept getting tortured. Sound familiar?"

"Wow," he said. "You're good."

"You're making this very difficult."

"Just doing my job."

"Harassment? Endangering my life? Nice job you've got there."

He stood, and walked over to the bed. Kate didn't seem alarmed, not even when he sat down next to her. "If you don't want to testify, I suppose there's not much I can do to force you. But I'd bet good money that

Baker's gonna run that picture, and when he does, you're going to need help."

"Now it's blackmail? Nice."

He studied her eyes. They were brown, a café au lait, and they were intelligent. Observant. And very attractive. He shifted his gaze down to her lips, and, once again, they were surprising. Not terribly lush, not like what was so popular right now, but they were smooth and perfect with her face. Altogether a remarkable looking woman who was working very hard to be as unremarkable as possible. "I can keep you safe."

"How?"

"Let me make some phone calls."

"Gonna call the cops?"

"Yeah."

She put her cup down on the rickety nightstand. "Tell me something. How do you have so much time to devote to little old me? Don't take this the wrong way, but I know your friend's death isn't the only crime this city has seen for two days."

"It's the only one I care about."

"So they just let you pick your cases?"

He smiled. "It's a little more complicated than that."

"I think I could follow along."

"I'll bet you could. If I could tell you."

"Detective Yarrow, I think you're full of crap. I have things to do. Coffee hour is over."

"This isn't a joke, Kate. These gangbangers'll kill you without a second thought."

She sighed. "Make your phone calls. Then let me know what you're offering."

"Good enough." He went to her door, but before

he left he turned once again. "I'm curious. This guy that's stalking you. How come you never reported him to the police."

"I did."

"No, you didn't. I looked."

"You looked in the wrong place. Now I really do have things to do."

Damn, he really did like her. He sincerely hoped she'd get out of this alive.

NATE AND SETH WERE QUIET in the elevator as they rode up to the roof of the downtown Los Angeles office of Omicron. It was just past seven, and most of the employees had gone home.

Nate went over the plan once more. He'd done everything possible to make sure this went off without a hitch, but he wouldn't relax until the job was finished.

They were walking into the lion's den. They had their fake work orders, he knew exactly where they were going to thread the fiber optic cable, just where to position the cameras and the microphones, but, still, anything could happen. The wrong person could ask the wrong questions, and that would be that. Operation over.

Not to mention they'd both end up dead.

But, just like every mission he'd taken on for the military, he wouldn't think about what could go wrong. Seth knew more about surveillance equipment than anyone Nate knew, and that was saying a lot.

He trusted the plan, and he trusted Seth. When they were finished they'd be able to see all of Leland Ingram's office and hear every word spoken. And, Nate was sure, Leland Ingram would lead them to the real prize. To the man who was the power behind Omicron.

It had to be someone high up the food chain. Someone who could get the millions of dollars necessary to run a covert operation of this magnitude. Someone who had the President's trust.

All the planning Nate had done over the past year would pay off, starting tonight. Nothing would go wrong. There was too much riding on success.

The elevator door opened. No one was on the roof. He looked at Seth. "Let's lock and load."

Seth grinned. "Roger that."

KATE GOT UP AT 6:10 a.m., feeling worse than she had when she went to bed. She'd slept with her gun under her pillow, although that's not what had kept her up.

She'd seriously considered every aspect of telling Yarrow what he wanted to know. But, in the end, she'd come to the conclusion that she had to keep her secret. Because if she told him any part of what she'd seen that day in the hotel, she'd have to testify eventually. And that would make her a sitting duck.

The picture in the paper, which she felt sure was going to happen, was bad enough. She had to disappear. This time, though, she wouldn't even dare stay in Los Angeles. She'd ask Nate to send her to Colorado, where she could work with Cade. Nate had told her Cade had a cabin no one would ever find. Or maybe she'd just go off on her own. Hell, she could be a waitress anywhere, right?

But she had to decide fast. At the very least, she had to leave this place. Ditch Yarrow and disappear. She'd call Nate at seven, and find out what intel he'd gathered.

Last night, he'd calmed her down somewhat, but they'd all agreed that her only recourse was to go where no one could find her.

She stepped into the shower, trying to recall one thing she'd read last night about her new history. Other than the fact that she had an older brother and a younger sister, which she'd had in her real life, nothing else had stuck.

The thought made her throat tighten. She tried so hard not to think of her family, but it was hardest when she was learning to be a new Kate. She adored her family and missed them so desperately that sometimes it felt as if it would kill her.

They all lived in Washington, D.C., so the odds of them seeing her picture were slim, but God, what if… She couldn't imagine what they'd think, how hurt they'd be if they realized she'd been alive all this time and never contacted them. Her father had a heart condition, and her biggest nightmare was that news of her covert life since Kosovo would kill him.

She forced herself to stop. Just stop. Thoughts of her family sent her into a deadly spiral of pain and regret, and there was too much at stake to go there. She turned off the shower and instantly went still when she heard banging on the front door.

Her stomach clenched as she grabbed a towel and got herself dry as quickly as she could. The banging got louder, and she wondered what new horror was about to enter her life.

She pulled her jeans up over still-damp thighs, which was a real treat. With her hair still wrapped in a towel and her T-shirt sticking to her skin, she tucked her gun into her ankle holster, then went to the door and looked through the peephole.

Yarrow. He was beating on the door like a madman, and when she opened the door, he almost fell inside the room.

"What?"

"Get your stuff together. Now."

"What? Why?"

"Do it. Don't argue."

He crossed the room and looked outside, down into the parking lot. His curse brought her next to him, and when she looked down she saw her car, totally engulfed in flames. Only then did she hear the distant sirens.

"Oh, my God." The car burned fast, as if it had been doused with an accelerant. A crowd was gathering and she wanted to shout at them to get away, that the gas tank could explode any minute. For a moment, she thought Omicron had found her, but that couldn't be. They'd never bother with burning her car unless she was in it. This was a warning from the gang that had killed Tim Purchase. "How did they find me?"

"It doesn't matter now. Pack," Yarrow said, shutting the drapes only to pull his cell out of his pocket.

Kate got her ass in gear. No matter what, she couldn't stay here. And now, she had no car. So she'd go with Yarrow until she could get in touch with Nate. At this rate, he wasn't going to ever get his work done. Not while he had to deal with one crisis after another on her behalf.

Of course, the box was the most important thing, but she focused first on her clothes. Good thing she didn't have many. As she emptied the closet, she heard Yarrow ask if the coast was clear. She wondered how good his men were. If it had been Nate or Seth, she wouldn't have worried; they would have checked every shadow. But the police? Sadly, she didn't have much faith there, but she also didn't have many options.

"What else?" he asked, his impatience making her more nervous.

She put the rest of her clothes in her suitcase, then went into the bathroom and collected her few belongings there. She dropped her towel and ran a quick brush through her wet hair, then went back to the bed. There, she saw her new papers sitting on the bedside table. She quickly put them back in the envelope and put them in her tote. "That's it. You get the suitcase."

He took it to the door, while she put on her coat, grabbed her tote and the box.

Yarrow called down once more, making sure everything was ready, then he hurried her into the dank hallway. At the bottom of the stairs, his car waited, running, the trunk open. She debated holding the box, but he'd have too many questions about it, so she put it in the trunk next to her suitcase. He slammed it shut, then she rushed to the passenger door, keeping her head low.

A man she didn't know shut her door, then pounded twice on the roof. Just then, the fire truck arrived, and Yarrow took off like a shot. She hunkered down, afraid someone with a camera phone would take her picture, take a picture of his car. They dodged a couple of black-and-whites, then they were on the street.

Three turns later, he slowed the car and Kate sat up straighter. "Where are we going?"

"Somewhere safe."

She turned to face the window so he wouldn't see her incredulity. There was nowhere safe.

Yarrow got out his cell once more. This time, he asked for Captain Emerson.

She listened carefully to his conversation and gathered that Yarrow was in trouble, not just for taking her from the motel, but for getting her picture in the paper in the first place.

She looked into the back seat, and there it was. The *Los Angeles Times*. She grabbed it, expecting her photo to be on page one, but she wasn't that important. In fact, she was on page three, and, lucky for her, the photo wasn't that big. You couldn't make out any of the details of her face, unless you knew what you were looking for.

The article itself said that she had been an employee at the hotel, and that she was a material witness. Great. Marvelous. There was no doubt at all that somehow Omicron would know it hadn't been Kate Rydell, but Katherine Ashman, the woman who had worked in the stuffy accounting office in Kosovo, dutifully adding up numbers and detailing her notes so that the U.N. could supervise the change of regimes. The woman, so young and inexperienced, who had first discovered a rogue CIA operation that involved selling illegal chemical weapons to other nations.

"All right," Yarrow said, putting his phone back in his jacket pocket.

"All right, what?"

"We've got a place to go."

"Where?"

He looked at her, then back at the road while he got onto the freeway. "A safe house."

"A safe house where?"

He sighed. "What difference does it make? It's safe. They won't find you there."

"It matters to me."

"Tujunga, okay?"

She looked at the paper on her lap and she had no energy to finish the article, so she stared out the window as the car slowed for traffic. She needed to call Nate, to make sure he knew where she was so he could get her. But there wasn't a thing she could do until she got the address.

"You okay?"

"What do you think?" she asked.

"I think this whole thing would go a lot easier if you told me who torched your car."

"I don't know."

"Sure you do. They're the same people who killed Tim."

She turned to him again. He was all rumpled, as if he'd run out of his house without bothering to check a mirror. His shirt was a pale blue, clean and ironed; the only thing on him that didn't look worn. His pants were as wrinkled as his jacket. It occurred to her that he hadn't come from home at all. He'd done as he'd promised and stuck to her twenty-four-seven. "You just don't give up, do you?"

"Nope. It drove my ex crazy."

"I can see why."

He looked at her with his odd blue eyes. "I get the job done."

"Too bad you're not out tracking the men who killed your friend."

His lips curled slightly. "I'm not the only persistent one in the car."

She didn't respond. Not for a long time. But she kept watching him, wondering how he was going to take it when she vanished. She felt bad for him. He'd keep trying, even though she knew once Nate got her out, Yarrow would never be able to find her. "Hey," she said.

"Hmm?"

"What's your name?"

He smiled at her again, this time with a little warmth behind it. "Vince."

She repeated it to herself. It seemed right. Maybe, when it was all over with Omicron, when she was Katherine once again, she'd get in touch with Vince Yarrow, and she'd apologize. But for now, her lies were the only thing standing between her and a very ugly death.

5

VINCE TURNED ON the familiar street, a little used road in an old section of Tujunga where his mother had lived for eighteen years. The old place looked like a dump— his fault. He should have made it a point to come out here more often. He was an only child, and, in her last years, his mother hadn't had many friends.

There'd been the regular visits from the home health workers, and from Meals on Wheels, but she'd been lonely. He'd known it. He hadn't done enough about it.

Now, after her death, he was here whenever he could find some time, boxing up her life to give to Goodwill. Getting ready to sell the place.

Kate hadn't said much. He kept thinking about who she was and what she was running from. Her reaction to the shooting had been way too calm for a woman with no violence in her past. So what was it? Had she gotten mixed up with drugs? Killers?

He still didn't buy the stalker theory, not totally, but there had been danger in her past. At least now he'd have her to himself, at least for a little while, and his intention was to get her defenses down. He didn't give a shit about her past. He was willing to bargain away her sins. He might be suspended, but he still had friends in the District Attorney's office. All he cared about was her testimony.

He turned into the bare driveway and stopped the car. There was no automatic garage opener here. He'd meant to put one in years ago. It was on his list of improvements. Way at the bottom of the list.

He got out, opened the garage, then drove into the dark space. A couple of rows of boxes, mostly clothes and linens, lined the side wall, but he'd barely scratched the surface. His mother had saved every damn thing she'd ever had.

"Is this your place?" Kate asked.

"No. It belonged to my mother."

"Where is she now?"

"Dead," he said, as he turned off the engine. "Let's go."

Kate got out of the car, and he opened the trunk before closing the garage. She pulled out her box, and he took her suitcase into the small house.

It had been a good size for his mom. One bedroom, plenty of closets, not a lot of places she'd have to clean. It was a perfect place to hide Kate. Not a lot of people knew about this place. His ex-wife, his boss, his partner. The real estate woman. That was about it. There was no phone, although he'd kept the cable TV.

He walked Kate down the long central hallway, not bothering to point out the living room, kitchen or bath. At the end of the house was the bedroom. Most of the weekends he spent here, he'd slept on the couch by the TV. But he'd tried out the bed a few times, and it was pretty damn comfortable. Hell, it was miles above the sleazy motel.

He watched Kate look around at the flowery room.

Bedspread, pillow shams, dust ruffle and curtains were all the same. Old-fashioned and sentimental, which was his mother to a *T*.

"The dresser and closet are both empty, so you can put your stuff away there."

"I'm not going to be here long enough to unpack," she said.

He put her suitcase on the bed. "No? Planning on leaving the country?"

"Don't be ridiculous. I just can't stay in your mother's house indefinitely. I have to find a job. I have to buy a car, remember?"

"Huh," he said. "Here I was, thinking you were pretty smart."

She put the box and her tote down by the closet door. When she turned to him, there was no amusement in her eyes. "I understand these people believe I saw them. And I understand that they want me not to testify. So as soon as you tell your reporter friend that I saw nothing and that I'm not going to testify, the problem will be solved."

He smiled. "Okay, not stupid. Just naive."

"Gee, I wonder why you're not married anymore?"

"It had nothing to do with my honesty."

"I assume there's a bathroom in this house?"

"Everything's off the hall. I'm going to make some coffee. I think there's some tea, somewhere."

"Coffee's fine. Thanks."

She left, and he was very tempted to go to the box of hers and see what was so precious. It wouldn't be a very nice thing to do, but was nice his objective?

Kate stepped back into the bedroom, giving him a

jolt. "I'd appreciate it if you'd stay out of this room as long as I'm your guest here."

"Hey."

"Honesty, remember? Isn't that how we're going to play it?"

"Okay, fine. Jeez."

She waited until he was in the hall, then she shut the door behind her. He headed for the kitchen, needing that coffee. He kept the house stocked with the basics, but not much more. Luckily, there was a local market that delivered. He'd have Kate put together a list of what she needed.

Meanwhile, he pondered the forbidden box as he counted out the coffee.

Kate locked the bathroom door, then turned on the water in the sink. She doubted Vince would eavesdrop, but she was taking no chances. With anything. She'd seen his interest in the box that held the ledgers, so she'd put a small piece of tape between the top and the base. If he snooped, she'd know.

She pressed Nate's speed dial, and waited as the phone rang. When she got his voice mail, she debated telling him her circumstances. It was never a good idea to leave a trail of any kind. Instead, she asked him to call her.

She thought about Yarrow, about why he'd brought her here instead of taking her to the police station. Of course, he wanted to break her. That was a given. And he wanted her to live so she could get on the stand. But his mother's house?

He probably didn't want her to see his place. That made sense. He didn't know her at all. And she had the feeling he thought she was a fugitive. She wondered what his reaction would be if she told him the truth.

It didn't matter. She wasn't saying a word. And she wasn't staying long. As soon as Nate called back, they'd figure out a way to spring her. The car was unfortunate. A new one would use up more of their precious resources. But she wasn't worried about the gang. She wouldn't be Kate Rydell any longer, and she wouldn't be living in L.A. At least not near downtown.

Maybe heading off to Colorado was the right move. She could forget all this and carry on with her work. She sat down on the edge of the bathtub. She had a bad headache, probably from all the adrenaline from this morning. She could have been killed.

It was odd how many times people had tried to kill her. Most people go their whole lives without that little pleasure. Not her. She wasn't a soldier, she wasn't a bad guy. She was just Kate, a forensic accountant, and yet she was marked for death, not just from a rogue CIA organization but now from a street gang. Neato.

How she wished it was all over. Her fantasies centered around going back to the world she'd once known, but in her saner moments she wondered if that would even be possible. She wasn't the same person, not by a long shot.

She trusted exactly six people. Well, that wasn't true because she trusted her family. But they thought she was dead, so she couldn't turn to them for help. Nope, her world consisted of the people she'd met in Kosovo, the people who were willing to sacrifice their lives to stop a terrible wrong.

It had started off so simply. Some discrepancies in the books. And because she'd been trained to search out every detail, she'd followed the trail. Right to Omicron.

They had created a chemical weapon, one that was as virulent and deadly as VX. It was easily transportable and completely odorless, and it would stick to whatever surface it touched. The real horror was that neither atropine or 2-PAM chloride worked as an antidote. The nerve agent could kill a tremendous number of people with a relatively small payload. And despite the ban on chemical warfare, Omicron had every intention of selling this stuff to some very nasty people. People who didn't have any qualms about genocide.

And when the truth had been discovered—by her, by Harper, by Nate's team—they'd had no qualms about killing those who'd found them out.

A knock on the door startled her. "Yes?"

"Coffee's ready."

"Thanks. I'll be right there." She stood, shoving her sadness away. Action was the best remedy for the heartsickness that threatened to overwhelm. She had to get back to those ledgers. To recreate the paper trail. But she couldn't do it with Vince on her tail. She had to get out.

After a dissatisfying glimpse of herself in the mirror, she left the bathroom in search of coffee. Vince had already fixed himself a cup and he was standing against the sink, watching the door. He'd put out cream and sugar and even a few packages of sugar substitute. Nice. Not nice enough to get her to betray her friends, but still.

She fixed herself a cup, then did a quick visual of the kitchen. Like the bedroom, it looked as if a little old woman had lived there. Teapots, which she found appealing, doilies and the omnipresent flowers on the curtains and the tablecloth. The room made her think of her grandmother's place. It was sweet, if a bit closed in.

"There's a notepad on the table. Write down what you need from the store, and I'll get it."

"I'm sure whatever you have is fine."

He pushed himself away from the sink and opened the fridge. "I doubt that. Unless you're into imported beer, mustard and really old leftover Chinese."

She looked for herself and saw he wasn't exaggerating. Then she went to the small pantry at the back wall, and there wasn't much to thrive on there, either. Some soup, mostly chicken and stars, some cans of assorted vegetables, lots of flour and baking soda. But nothing that was easy and neat. "Fine. I'll write a few things down."

"Plan for the week." Vince finished his coffee and poured himself a second cup.

"A few days, at the most."

He didn't look at her as he put the coffeepot back. "You know how long I've been working the gang unit?"

"No," she said, not wanting to hear this lecture. She sat down by the notepad and tried to think of what she wanted him to buy. The temptation was to list terribly expensive things just to be arbitrary, but she wouldn't. He was, after all, simply doing his job.

"Three years. It's a long time. Most cops get out after a year. If they last that long."

"Uh-huh."

"You know why?"

She looked up. "Because gangs are violent, have laws unto themselves, and they don't care who they kill."

"That's about right. They take pride in killing. Anyone outside their personal gang is fair game. And they don't tend to notice the finer details, either. Even if the cover of tomorrow's *Times* included sworn affidavits that you didn't see a thing and that you'd never testify, they would come after you. They *will* come after you. They won't stop until you're dead. That's not conjecture. It's fact."

"They can't kill me if they can't find me."

"There are gangs in every state of the union. There's no place you can hide."

"That's not true, and you know it. Listen, Vince. I hope it's okay to call you that, but since I'm giving you my grocery list…"

"Vince is fine."

"You don't have to lie to me. I understand I'm in danger. I also understand that it's you who put me here. So pardon me if I don't exactly trust you to be my personal hero. I know what you want, and I can't give it to you. That's not going to change, even if that gang were right outside."

He sat down across from her. "That makes me very sad, Kate. Because Tim deserves better."

"Hey, I'm sorry you lost your friend."

"He wasn't just a friend. He was my personal hero. One of them, at least. He was actually making a difference out there. Hundreds of kids were choosing not to be in gangs. They would pile into his crappy building and do their homework, or play ball or just talk. They liked him and they believed in him, and some of them got killed for it. But he kept fighting. They'd tried to kill him before, but man, he figured he was bulletproof. Of course, now we know he was wrong. His wife, who, by the way, is a really nice lady, is going to try to continue his work, but I don't think she'll have much luck. Those kids, they were there because of Tim. He had a way about him."

She stared at the paper in front of her, unwilling to meet Vince's gaze.

"So all those kids, the ones who would have been going to Tim's place, are gonna end up in the gangs. And most of them are gonna end up dead."

"I can't help that."

"No, but you can take a stand. If we can convict those who are responsible, some of those kids will continue to fight. Not many, but enough. And maybe one of those kids will pick up Tim's message."

"What about you?"

"Me? Nah. Once this is done, I'm out."

"What do you mean?"

"I mean I'm out. Done. I'm giving them back my badge."

"Why? It's clear you're impassioned about this. That you care deeply."

"Not anymore."

"What will you do?"

"No idea. I thought about getting a little boat. Maybe take tourists out fishing."

"I don't believe it. I think you care too much to walk away."

"Kate, I hate to tell you, but I don't care what you believe. I just care that you tell me the truth."

She sighed. Then started filling out her list. Tea, of course. Milk. Cereal. Some fresh fruits and vegetables. She loved to cook, and she had several favorites she'd learned to make in Kosovo, but she didn't put down any of the exotic ingredients. So she listed things that were simple—pasta, chicken, hamburger. Things he'd use once she was gone.

Vince's cell phone rang and he took it out of his pocket. "Yarrow."

She kept putting down food items, but she also listened. It wasn't easy to make sense of everything, since Yarrow was pretty cryptic, but she gathered that it was his partner and that the news wasn't terribly good. There was mention of Baker and of the Captain. Vince's frown confirmed her impressions.

He hung up, but he didn't put the phone away. "You about finished?"

She nodded. Whatever she'd forgotten, she could live without.

He went to the sideboard and pulled a phone book from the bottom of a stack of books. She couldn't see what he looked up, but when he called, then said he wanted to place an order, she knew it was the grocery store. One that delivered.

Damn, she'd figured she'd have some maneuvering room when he went shopping. It didn't matter. The guys would get her out cleanly, especially now that she had his address. They were very good at that kind of thing.

She handed him the list, then took her coffee into the living room. The only thing relatively new in the place was the TV. The couches and the coffee table all looked decades old and worn. There were a couple of pictures on the wall, the kind most often found in motel chains. The curtains were dull and dusty, as was the carpet. It was a sad room, not even counting the two empty beer bottles leaning against the bottom of the couch.

The pictures on the fireplace mantel drew her attention. Vince must have been an only child. There he was as a toddler and as a teenager in a baseball uniform. He'd been an adorable kid and an even better looking young man. She looked back at him in the kitchen. He still was handsome as hell. Of course, it would be interesting to see him all cleaned up, but even so she could see the appeal.

Something shifted inside, and it took a moment for her to recognize the feeling. It was interest. And it was all sexual. Wow, it had been a long time since that had come her way.

Of course, she wouldn't do a thing about it. But it was fascinating, nonetheless. She'd forgotten how it felt. Which was probably for the best. She couldn't get close to anyone. Not for any reason. Especially not just to scratch that particular itch.

But it didn't hurt to think about it, if only for a moment.

When he looked up at her, she turned away. No, she was wrong. Even a moment was too long.

VINCE PUT HIS CELL AWAY. He wished he'd packed all the pictures. They were personal, and the way Kate was studying them made him uncomfortable.

What was it going to take to break her? He didn't want to cause her pain, but dammit. He had to know what she knew. If he could just get inside that wall of hers. Everything she did was measured and controlled. So careful, it was as if she expected landmines under the carpet.

He walked through the kitchen into the laundry room, and he shut the door behind him. Then he got out his cell and hit Redial. When the nice lady answered, he added a few things to his order. Red wine. White wine. Bourbon. Vodka. And just in case, a fifth of tequila.

Who knows? It might even work. And if it didn't? He wouldn't care half so much.

6

HE LAY ON THE COUCH, listening to the quiet of the house, thinking about the woman in the bedroom. Kate intrigued him. Not just because she had something he wanted, either. He'd always loved a mystery, and man, she was nothing but secrets.

Dinner had been odd but interesting. He'd fixed his famous spaghetti and sausage, and she'd made a salad. The wine, a damn good chardonnay, had been less than successful. She'd had one glass, no more. And while he'd turned on the charm and used all the subtle inter-rogation tricks in his arsenal, she hadn't given an inch.

He had no idea where she came from, who her family was. She'd been just as cryptic about her supposed stalker and why she was so determined to live under the radar. Damn. Talk about a hard nut to crack.

All she'd really succeeded in doing was making him more curious. And more determined.

Just the way she ate made him crazy. Little bites between even, white teeth. Totally controlled and in the Continental style. Had she lived in Europe? Was she even an American citizen?

And then there was the way she looked at him. No dodging, no sweating, no tells at all. Even though he knew beyond any shadow of a doubt that she was lying, none of her body language gave it away. How had she learned that? Was she actually a grifter? The only people he'd known who could do that as convincingly were con artists of the highest order. But he didn't get that vibe off Kate, although that could just mean she was extraordinarily good at her job.

But why would she live in a dive of a motel or work for room service, for that matter? No con artist he'd ever known would go that far undercover.

Vince sat up, the quilt falling off the couch with his sudden move. *She was undercover.* Shit, why hadn't he realized that before? Probably for Interpol, which would explain the whole eating thing. And that's why she couldn't testify.

He got off the couch and started pacing. It was dark in the room, but he knew the space so well he didn't need to turn on a light. His thoughts tumbled all over themselves as piece after piece of Kate's puzzle came together.

It all made sense. He had no idea what she could be investigating, but there had to be some kind of cooperation between agencies, even if the agency was overseas. Yes, that had to be it. He'd talk to her—she wouldn't need to blow her cover. Something could be done, and she could tell him what he needed to know, and then—

Even if she had seen the killers, she wouldn't be able to give him more than general descriptions, but that would be enough. He'd know what gang they were from, and he knew how to put the pressure on. He'd get there, he would. He just had to make sure Kate came clean.

IT WAS JUST AFTER SEVEN, and Kate had to get her act together. She needed a shower, she needed breakfast, and she needed Nate to get off his ass and get her out of here.

She gathered her clothes and bath supplies and headed for the bathroom. Although the bed had been comfortable, she hadn't slept well. A new place was always disconcerting, but, more than that, she couldn't stop thinking about the man in the living room.

She'd actually had a nice evening. He'd been a charming and considerate host, and he hadn't even pressed her too much. He couldn't help asking questions, but when she'd sidestepped each one, he'd had the decency to let it slide. Today, of course, could be quite a different matter. Who knew what he'd do to get what he wanted?

If only she'd hear from Nate. They had to have a plan, and time was running out. The longer she stayed with Vince, the greater the chances the gang would discover her whereabouts. Not to mention the repercussions from the photo. Did Omicron already know? Had they figured out that Kate Rydell was actually Katherine Ashman?

She didn't hear anything from the living room, so maybe he was still sleeping. She'd call Nate again from the bathroom, even though it was early. He'd be grumpy, but too bad. There was too much—

She stopped, startled, as she saw the bathroom was already occupied by a seminaked Vince Yarrow, with shaving lotion on half his face. Her gaze moved down to his chest, all broad and tanned and nicely muscled, and then down a bit more to the unbuttoned jeans riding low on his slim hips.

"Morning."

Jerking her eyes up guiltily, she cleared her throat

and tugged at her belt. "Sorry. Just let me know when you're done."

"There's coffee made."

She smiled, willing the heat from her face. "Great. Thanks."

Vince returned to shaving and she walked quickly to the kitchen. Once there, she put her bath things on the counter and fixed herself a mug.

Boy, she hadn't been prepared for that little trip to libido land. She already knew he was pretty hot, but she'd had no idea he looked like that. *Mama.*

Okay, it was officially too long since she'd had any kind of sex. She'd barely even acknowledged sex existed. Not for her, anyway.

Seeing Christie and Boone fall for each other had been sweet, but kind of like watching a movie. It had had nothing to do with her, and it hadn't touched her at all.

In her own defense, it was hard to think about dating when people were trying to kill you. And when you couldn't possibly tell the truth about anything in your life. So, yeah, she'd cut herself some slack and hadn't thought about it. Until now.

He had just the right amount of hair on his chest. Dark, curly, it showed off his muscles very nicely. She especially liked the narrow trail that slipped beneath his jeans.

She took a drink of coffee and gasped as it burnt the roof of her mouth. She cursed, then put the mug on the table.

A low, slow chuckle made her turn. Vince stood in the doorway, now shaved and fully dressed. At least his T-shirt was on the tight side. "Why, Kate. Such language."

"I know a lot more, so don't get me started."

"Me? I'd never dream of it. Bathroom's all yours."

"Thanks." She gathered her few things, and the mug, then headed out.

"You like pancakes?" he asked, just as she hit the door.

"They're okay."

"I'll cook us up a batch."

"I'm just as happy with cold cereal, so don't go to any trouble for me."

"Don't worry, I'm not."

"Okay, then," she said.

"Okay."

"And Kate?"

"Yeah?"

"My eyes are up here."

She jerked her head up, then spun on her heels. She was so busted. God, she hadn't even realized she'd been staring like that. And not just at his chest.

The minute she closed the bathroom door behind her, she used all the swear words she knew, some of them twice.

DESPITE HIS EXHAUSTION, Nate wheeled the old Cutlass toward home in a convoluted route that he varied regularly. Except for the rush hour traffic he had to fight, he was glad he'd finished work early so he could take it easy tonight. He needed sleep desperately. It was difficult to concentrate on his security business while there was so much to be done now that the Omicron bugs were in place. But the money had to come from somewhere.

He pulled in to the driveway that led to the garage behind his tiny house. He got his cell phone out and dialed Peter, the man for whom he'd subcontracted today's security installation, and waited.

The machine answered, and after the beep he said, "Job's done, Pete. It's about four-fifteen and I'm home for the night. I'll see you tomorrow about the money. 'Night." He disconnected and climbed out of the car.

Automatically, he checked the pair of windows as he passed them on the way to the front door. Since the small rental had no back door, even in inclement weather he had to make his way around. On the plus side, with only four windows and one door, it was a lot easier to maintain security.

He opened the door and went in, immediately opening two of the windows to get a cross breeze. He turned on his coffeemaker and the small TV that sat on his makeshift desk.

As the savory smell of coffee permeated his rooms, he wrote out the bill for Peter, carefully noting the hours and the various devices he'd installed, including several hundred feet of Belden multipair cable. When the bill was complete, he put it in an envelope and set it to the side.

He opened his laptop, running now on house power, and entered the password that would allow him to play back everything the Omicron bug had picked up. He turned the volume up and went to pour a cup of coffee.

His thoughts turned to Kate and how he was going to get her from the detective's house as he filtered through what he was hearing on the tape. So far nothing sounded out of the ordinary—just the usual chatter that went on in offices.

He took out the map of Tujunga, sipping his coffee and letting the stress of the day ease from his back and shoulders as he went through different scenarios and various routes. Kate said the detective was sharp, that it wouldn't be easy to fool him, so they'd probably have to drug him. Not Nate's favorite method, but they had to get Kate out.

He was close to stopping for the night when something caught his attention. He ran the recording back to the start.

Suddenly he was wide awake. "Shit," he said. He stopped the playback again and pulled out his cell phone. A minute later Seth was on the line.

"I got something," Nate said.

"What?"

"They've got a warehouse. A storage facility."

"Jesus, man. Where?"

Nate chewed his lower lip. "City of Industry. I don't have an address, though."

"Hey, if we can find it, we can expose those bastards."

"It's worth a try. Just knowing they've made enough of that crap to need a warehouse… We've got to move on this."

There was a moment of silence from Seth's end. "Can you save just that conversation?"

"Sure."

"Let's do that and sleep on it," Seth said. "We'll figure something out. After we get Kate."

"That stuff can kill one hell of a lot of people, Seth."

"Not if we get the bastards first."

KATE WAS IN THE KITCHEN, cooking something that smelled great. He'd offered to help, but she'd chased him away. It was nice.

She'd been quiet today, and he hadn't yet figured out

how to bring up the whole undercover thing. The more he thought about it, though, the more convinced he became that he'd figured her out.

He thought again about that box of stuff she guarded so carefully. He needed to see what was in there, but even he realized that would be a major invasion of her privacy. Besides, he wanted her as an ally, not an enemy.

He turned on his laptop and checked his e-mail. There was a note there from Tim's wife. He opened it, afraid of what she had to say, but she just wanted to let him know about the funeral.

God, he didn't want to go to that. Of course, he had to. Not just to pay his respects, but to see who else showed up. It was quite possible that the killers would come to gloat. At the very least, Vince could question whoever showed up to see if they'd heard anything.

It was odd that the killers hadn't taken credit for the job. Most of the gangs he knew so well would have used the murder for their own aggrandizement. Either telling tales around the crack pipe or boasting in graffiti on the walls of the city. Someone had to know who'd pulled the trigger. Aside from Kate, that was.

He answered Liz Purchase, then quickly went through the rest of his mail. One e-mail stopped him. It was from George, Tim's assistant. According to him, gang violence since Tim's death was out of control. Six deaths, four drive-bys and at least four armed robberies, all attributable to gangs who'd been quiet for a long while. Most of them were believed to be in disputes over Tim's territory. Attendance at Purchase House was down to almost nothing, and George was debating closing the doors for good.

Vince shut the computer off without answering. All this shit was raining down on the city, and here he was playing house. He should forget about protecting her. Maybe the smart thing to do was to cut her loose, then trail her. When the gang came to kill her, he'd know. Of course, that was taking a pretty big chance with her life. But goddammit, kids were dying out there. Lots of them. And if she wouldn't help voluntarily, maybe he needed to take away her options.

"Okay," Kate said, calling to him from the kitchen. "Dinner."

He looked at the door, picturing her in her jeans and her sweater, her long dark hair so shiny on her shoulders. She was a beautiful woman, and he wished like hell he'd met her some other way. He could tell she didn't find him repulsive or anything. Not the way she kept staring at him, stealing looks when she thought he couldn't see.

Hell, the wine hadn't worked. The pleading had been a bust. Maybe the answer lay between the sheets. The idea held plenty of appeal.

He headed to the kitchen where Kate had set the table. She was at the stove, taking out a casserole dish. She smiled at him as she put it down on a waiting trivet. "How about you get us some drinks."

"White wine?"

"Sure," she said. "But I'm not going to have more than one glass."

"You don't like pinot?"

She put her hands on her hips. "You aren't going to get me drunk so I'll talk."

"Hey."

"Don't even try to deny it. You're about as subtle as a Mack truck."

"Fine. Have it your way. But it wouldn't kill you to relax a little. You've been through a lot."

"Thanks. Your compassion is touching."

He walked closer and put his hand on her arm. "Believe it or not, I can be a nice guy. Not often, mind you, but from time to time."

She didn't move or look away. That straightforward stare had him wishing that he'd had no ulterior motives. God damn, she was beautiful.

"Wine," she said, her voice soft and deep.

He moved his hand down her arm, squeezing her gently. When he let go, he heard her take a sharp breath. The moment was over quickly, though, with her getting the salad from the counter and setting it on the table.

He busied himself with the wine, and a few moments later, they were seated. The food, a chicken and rice concoction, smelled great. For the first time since this morning, she had trouble looking at him. It was a start.

After dinner, he'd put on some music, build a fire. Who knows, maybe the combination would help break down some of her walls. And when the time was right, he'd ask her who she was working for. Tell her he knew she was undercover.

It would be fascinating to see her response. Of course, there wasn't much about her that he didn't find fascinating.

7

KATE TOOK ANOTHER sip of wine as she watched him eat. She hadn't been sure about his intentions until he'd reacted, but his quick denial said it all. The awful thing was, she completely understood his desperation. She knew what it was to feel helpless against such an incredible wrong, and how the need to make it right could consume every waking thought.

They were alike in so many ways. Vince reminded her of her father. In his younger days, he'd been an activist against the Vietnam War, and his passion and dedication had changed people's lives. And, like Vince, her father had never made a production of his cause. He'd simply done the work—all the things that most people didn't want to bother with. Making the phone calls, getting the word out, fighting the battle through logic and tenacity. She'd learned about his struggles through others. Her mother, her uncle. Never from her father.

It impressed her that Vince had stuck it out in the gang unit for three years. She was no expert, but she knew enough about L.A. street gangs to understand the kind of courage and sacrifice it took to face that nightmare every day. She didn't believe he'd quit, either. Not him. He was too young, and his passion ran too deep.

"What are you smiling about?"

"Nothing," she said, not realizing she had been. "This is good wine."

He picked up the bottle and poured a little more into her glass. "I'm actually more of a whiskey guy, myself. But wine's good every once in a while."

"Whiskey, huh? That makes sense."

"Why?"

"You tough guys like that hard stuff."

He shook his head. "I just like the fact that I can go from zero to blasted in about five minutes."

"Blasted, huh? You do that often?"

"Not as often as I'd like. Hangovers are hell when you carry a gun."

"I'll bet."

He finished off the casserole on his plate, then put his fork down. It felt good that he'd liked her cooking. She used to enjoy her time in the kitchen, especially in Kosovo, where the women had taught her to make the local delicacies. Since she'd been on the run, she hadn't had many opportunities to cook. Even if she had the time, she mostly didn't have the money to buy anything decent.

Cooking was just one of a hundred things she missed. And being here with Vince had awakened yet another loss. She missed men. Not that she didn't see a lot of Nate and Seth, but they were comrades in arms, not dates. Not lovers. Not anymore.

She and Nate had only gone out for a little while. Then the shit had hit the fan and it became all business. Back in the States, she'd believed him to be dead for over a year, and when he'd turned out to be alive she'd realized again that their brief affair wouldn't have gone anywhere, even if things had gone down differently.

No, while she loved and admired Nate, he wasn't for her. He was, at the core, a man with huge appetites. He needed the danger as most men need to breathe. His appetite for women was just as voracious.

She wanted something quieter and deeper.

"You okay?"

She found she was looking at Vince, although she hadn't actually seen him. "I'm fine. I'll just do up the dishes." She stood and took his plate and hers to the sink.

"Wait a minute," he said, standing, too. "You cooked, I clean."

"It's okay. Really."

He came up beside her and grabbed a dishcloth from the counter. "I'll dry."

She nodded. "Fine."

"You want to tell me what that was about?"

"It was nothing. I'm fine."

"I know, but you also looked incredibly sad. I hope it wasn't anything I said."

"Not at all. Hiding out from killers with a man who'll stop at nothing to get what he wants couldn't be nicer. Honest."

He laughed, and she was glad because she'd meant to lighten things up. Melancholy was not a place she could afford to go.

He went to the table and brought back more dishes. For the next while they busied themselves with straightening up, and she even finished her wine. She also couldn't help but notice how close he stood. How big his hands were, how tanned against the white dishcloth.

He smelled good, too. Masculine. Sexy.

With no warning at all, the weight of her loneliness crushed her chest. Every night she'd slept alone in a strange bed, every solitary meal eaten in hiding, it all rushed at her in a wave of aching despair. She'd lost everything, *everything.* Could she steal one night to remind herself who'd she'd been? That once upon a time, she'd loved the feel of a man inside her?

The sound of the plate she'd been washing shattering in the sink made her jerk back, and then his hand was on her shoulder, turning her around.

"Kate?"

She looked at him, trying to mask it all, to smile so he wouldn't know that she was shattering, too. She failed miserably as her eyes welled and her lips trembled. This was all wrong. She had to be strong, invulnerable.

"What's wrong? What happened?"

She tore herself out of his grip and turned away, humiliation making her tears come faster. No one was supposed to see this part. Especially not him.

"Dammit, what's happening? Did I say something? I'm sorry if I did. I can be a total moron, really. Just ask my ex-wife."

She shook her head, but she still couldn't speak. Her throat felt swollen and her whole body ached with the sobs she was holding in.

His hands came back to her shoulders. "This is nuts," he said, pulling her toward him. "Talk to me."

She spun around, surprising him, and she wanted to tell him that she was all right, that she just needed— God, how she needed. With tears streaming down her face, she did the only thing she could. She lifted her chin, took him by the arms and pulled him down into a kiss.

He seemed frozen at first, but a second later he kissed her back. The moment his lips parted, she was desperate for more. To taste him, to feel him, it was all that was keeping her sane.

His body forced her against the sink, and she felt his cock beneath his jeans. Her hands moved to his back where she stroked him. She wasn't crying anymore, and her trembling had nothing to do with emptiness. He would fill her. He would take her back to another time, when she was Katherine and she was happy.

She needed to feel his skin so she tore at his T-shirt, pulling it out of his jeans so her hands could slide over his smooth, warm flesh.

His moan made her thrust with her hips and her tongue. When he pulled at her sweater she forced herself to let him go, to lift her arms, and once it was off, she reached behind to unclasp her bra. Vince pushed the straps off her shoulders, and her ugly white bra fell away.

She closed her eyes, feeling the air on her naked breasts. When he came back to her, his shirt was gone, too, and she sighed when she rubbed against his chest.

He swallowed her up with his arms, with his mouth, and that's exactly what she wanted. To disappear inside him and forget everything else.

The hair on his chest was soft but his small nipples were as hard as her own. His kisses were skillful and urgent, and the sounds he made were low and rough, the sounds of sex, which she hadn't heard in so long.

He ripped his mouth from hers only to find her neck,

where he licked and sucked and bit her, and it was perfect because she wanted to be devoured, swallowed whole.

Her hands moved down his back, and then slid over his sides until she found the waistband of his jeans. It wasn't easy to undo the buttons, to find the zipper and pull it down, not while he was touching her everywhere, squeezing her breasts and brushing her nipples with his broad palms. But somehow, she reached inside and found the fly of his boxers. Behind that, his cock. She circled him with her hand, feeling the heat and the weight of him, the slick moisture at the top and the straining of the shaft.

"God almighty, I can't—" He moaned as she pumped him, growing in her hand. With her eyes closed and his hard cock in her grasp it was easy to pretend that this was more than just scratching an itch. In the dark, he was not just a beautiful man who wanted her for his own reasons, but a man who wanted *her.* If she kept her eyes shut, she wouldn't be Kate.

He pulled his head back and gasped as her fingers squeezed him. His hand circled her wrist, holding her still. "Stop."

"No."

"You have to stop."

His pleading got through to her. If she didn't let him go, it would all be over, and she wasn't ready. Not nearly. So she pulled her hand away.

"Kate," he said.

She didn't want to see. Not yet.

"Kate, look at me."

She opened her eyes, knowing she was losing something necessary. Something that would hurt when she thought of it again. He had crouched a bit so that his eyes were level with her own. It wasn't so bad. He wanted her. The blue had almost disappeared behind the dark pupils. There was no mistaking his hunger.

"Come with me."

"Where?"

He smiled. "To the bedroom."

She was afraid that the short walk would dispel the fantasy, but how could she tell him that?

"I want to see you," he said. "I want you naked."

She nodded, but she didn't move.

"God, you're so beautiful. I can't—" He shook his head, stood tall and pulled her into a scorching kiss. As he stroked and teased her with his tongue, he squeezed her bottom, then he lifted her off her feet.

She cried out, latching on to his neck with her arms and his hips with her legs. Holding her, still kissing her, he headed toward the hallway.

She didn't even mind when he bumped her back against the wall, or that he had to pull away so he could maneuver. She just buried her face in his neck, breathing deeply and tasting everything she could.

He stopped, and she let her legs drop. When she looked up at him, he was smiling. Gently, he put her arms down to her sides. Then he undid the top button of her jeans.

She touched his hair as he bent to pull down her zipper and then her pants. Halfway there, he kissed her, right above the band of her panties, just below her navel.

After one more sharp tug, her pants pooled by her feet and she stepped out of them. He put his thumbs under the side band of her underwear and then they were off, too.

His sigh was loud and his breath warm just before he stood up again. She toed off her shoes and socks as he stripped himself bare.

There, that was it. The way he looked at her. He was her lover and he wanted her desperately, and she wanted him right back. Nothing but heat and want allowed, and she fell happily into this new moment.

His body was stunning. Everything from head to toe pleased her. His chest, his slim hips, the way his cock jerked when he touched her cheek.

He stepped closer. His arms circled her shoulders and he brought her flush against his body.

For a long moment, she simply reveled in the connection. How warm he was, how broad his shoulders. He kissed her gently, swept his tongue over her bottom lip, then he bent and lifted her once more. This time, he put her right back down on the bed, her head on the pillow.

He didn't join her right away. First, he looked at her, slowly, his gaze painting every inch of her skin.

She felt wanton, glorious and she parted her legs for him, wanting him to see how badly she ached.

"Oh, God," he whispered as he climbed on the bed. He kissed her again, taking his time, learning everything he could, and she learned him right back. The shape of his teeth, the way he breathed through his nose, and how when she moaned, he shivered.

Soon, though, he moved down, using the same skill, the same patience, to discover the rest of her. Not just her breasts, although he seemed to like them especially, but the curve of her neck and the taste of her inner arm.

She was in heaven behind her closed eyes, letting the

sensations have her. When he moved between her legs, she spread herself wider, wanting everything there was.

He spread her lips with his thumbs. A hot breath gave her gooseflesh, but it was his tongue, hardened to a point and deadly accurate, that took her to the edge.

She held on to the bed, then to his hair, then back to the bed, pulling the comforter as he kept up the perfect circles right on her clit, pressing slowly harder, getting faster and faster until every muscle in her body was strained to the limit. He didn't let up, not even when she pulled his hair hard, and then she came, the spasms jerking her body, the release so powerful she couldn't even breathe.

She hadn't even stopped shuddering when his knees moved under her legs, when his hands moved her feet around to his back. He was over her now, his breath hot and rapid on her face. Then his cock was pushing inside her, filling her slowly until he could go no farther.

She opened her eyes, needing to see him. And when she met his gaze, she squeezed.

His mouth opened on a silent scream, a bead of sweat dropped onto her temple. He moved. Pulled back. Thrust deep. Hard. So hard the whole bed moved. So hard she bit her own lip and didn't even feel it.

The whole time, he stared into her eyes. He never looked away, and she didn't blink and they were alone, the two of them, in all the world, and they were connected, and they were both trembling.

When he came, he cried out, a low bellow that was everything primal. Perfect. She closed her eyes once more, holding on to the moment, squeezing him close, fighting to stay right there.

But it didn't last forever.

He fell beside her, panting. She pulled her legs together, still feeling the ache where he'd been. Just that fast, he ceased to be her lover. It wasn't making love. And she was emptier than before.

NATE STARED AT HIS COMPUTER screen, not quite believing what he was seeing. He'd already listened to the audio about fifty times, and now was studying the video feed. Although the camera position was a little high, it did capture the surface of Leland Ingram's desk.

He'd been tailing Leland for a long time, and he'd discovered a lot about the man. He was married, but his wife was having an affair with her writing teacher. Leland had no clue. He also had no clue that his daughter, the light of his life, was a regular cocaine user. It would have killed her old man to find out, but the girl was crafty.

Leland spent most of his waking hours at Omicron. He wasn't the top man there, not by a long shot, but he was in charge of most of the dirty work. Nate had no proof, but he knew without doubt that it was Ingram who had put out the orders to kill Nate's team in Kosovo. Now, in addition to the bombshell about the secure facility, there was this.

On the corner of his desk was a copy of the *Los Angeles Times*. It was open to page three. To the picture and article about Kate Rydell, a material witness in the brutal slaying of antigang activist Tim Purchase.

Kate's picture was circled. There was no note attached. Ingram hadn't mentioned it once. But the picture was there, and that was bad.

He thought about calling Kate, but he didn't want to rush things. For the moment, Nate couldn't think of where to take her that would be safer.

She could stay with him, but it wouldn't be easy, and he'd have to leave her too often. Same with Seth. He didn't want her alone, not for a minute.

So maybe staying with the cop wasn't such a bad thing. He knew, given enough time, that Ingram could find out anything, including the address of Detective Yarrow's deceased mother. But for the immediate future, Kate was reasonably safe.

She'd told him that only three people knew about the house. He had to believe that none of them were connected to Omicron. Why would they be? The police force was local. They were small fry compared with Omicron.

The only thing that made sense was to get Kate out of L.A. He'd contact Cade tomorrow and start putting the wheels in motion to get Kate away.

But, he realized, she had to know. She had to be on her guard. There was no choice.

He looked at the clock. It was almost eleven. No need to bother her tonight. Tomorrow, he'd tell her. He hoped like hell she was getting a good night's rest. She'd need it.

KATE HAD HER EYES CLOSED while her breathing calmed, next to him on the bed. Her hair was a wild mess all over the pillow. Vince, propped up on his arm, let his gaze move slowly from her long legs to her smooth, flat belly, to the rise and fall of her breasts. He lingered there for a moment, thinking of how she'd tasted, how it had felt to tease that nipple with his tongue until it was ripe and hard.

It had been a long time for him. He'd been so optimistic, bringing the box of condoms here, but they'd sat in the drawer, unopened for the last three months. Before that, he'd had a couple of encounters, nothing to write home about. Nothing like Kate.

Shit, he wished things were different. If she'd just tell him the truth, they could figure things out. Get things moving in the right direction.

Well, that was pretty optimistic, too. Why would she want someone like him? Burnt out, obsessive, with no idea what he was going to do with his life. And if she was working for Interpol, then she didn't even live in this country, so...

Jesus, what the hell? He sat up, wishing he hadn't given up smoking.

Kate stirred, and the first thing she did was pull up the sheet to cover her body. "What's wrong?"

"Nothing. I thought you might like something to drink."

She nodded, then let her head fall back. "Juice would be great."

"Juice it is," he said. He got up and headed to the kitchen, grabbing his old blue robe from the back of the door on his way out. He stopped by the bathroom for a minute, then got the carton of OJ out of the fridge. He grabbed two glasses and headed back.

The whole time, he debated bringing up her undercover work. Maybe now wasn't the best time. It could wait till morning. She wasn't going anywhere.

The real question was, did he stay with her? In the bed? Did she want him to? Would they get any sleep? Damn, she looked so good lying there like that. She was so beautiful... He could still feel her legs wrapped around his waist as he buried himself inside her. Jesus. He was getting hard again. He hadn't known he still had it in him.

"Oh, thank you," she said, pulling herself up, and putting the pillow behind her back. He wished she hadn't pulled up that sheet.

But it was late, and it was cold, so he put the glasses and juice down, then pulled the rest of the covers up to her waist. Her smile made his cock jump, but he paid no attention to it. He'd let her call the shots for the rest of the night. If he got the feeling she wanted to be alone, he'd make a quiet exit. If she wanted him to stay, that would be just fine.

She poured them each some juice, and when she didn't tell him to leave he went around the bed and sat down on top of the covers.

"That was very wonderful," she said. "Thank you."

He couldn't help it. He laughed out loud.

"What's so funny?"

"Nothing. You're right. It was very wonderful."

"You're laughing at me."

"No, I'm not. Trust me."

She didn't look altogether convinced, but she let it go. "What time is it?"

He checked the clock on the bedside table. "Closing in on midnight."

"Is that all? I thought it was later."

"Tired?"

She nodded. "I think I'm going to sleep really well tonight."

"Good."

She looked down, then back at him. "You're welcome to stay. Or not. Whatever makes you comfortable."

He shifted, wanting to see more of her face, but when he did, he didn't like what he saw. She wanted him to go. It was there in the way she wouldn't meet his gaze. The downward tilt of her lips. "You're tired, and I snore like a madman. I'll let you get some rest," he said, standing up, not letting her see his disappointment.

"That's probably for the best," she said.

"Okay, well, good night." He walked to the door. "Is there anything else? You need something?"

"No, I'm good."

He nodded, smiled, then walked into the hall, closing the door behind him. He went to the living room and looked at the couch. He'd slept on it many times, but it had never looked so uninviting.

He sat down, wondering what the hell had just happened. He couldn't remember a better time. Not in bed. She'd been amazing, and goddammit, she'd been right there with him. So what had gone wrong?

Maybe he was just being a sentimental fool. She'd been horny. He'd been the only guy available. It was probably true, but it didn't feel right.

What was it about Kate Rydell? What didn't he see?

8

THE HARDER SHE TRIED to stop crying, the worse it got and even though she buried her head in the pillow, she was sure her sobs could be heard throughout the house. Thank goodness Vince was sleeping.

She never should have slept with him. The moment he'd walked out the door she'd felt horrible. Sadness filled her so intensely she thought she might go mad.

Her chest ached, her face hurt, her muscles strained and still she kept crying, weeping for all she'd lost, all she might never have again. There was so much wrong with every part of her life, and dammit, it had felt amazing to be with Vince. The way he'd kissed her, the way he'd touched her. It wasn't like she remembered at all—it was a thousand times better.

He'd been gentle and firm and sweet and hot and all the things her body had ached for. But mostly it was the way he'd kissed. God, she'd missed it so much.

And then it had gone to hell. The reality of her situation, the hopelessness of it all.

Some part of her had wanted him to stay the night. She'd wanted to feel his body next to hers. To spoon with him and to feel his sigh on her shoulder. She'd wanted to wake up next to him and to see him smile in that hazy, early morning warmth.

But she'd known, even before the sadness had fully hit, that to let him stay would have been torture. Never before had she lied to someone in her bed. She'd never had to, and it was horrible. She wasn't cut out for this. Not her.

Nothing in her life had prepared her for this kind of deceit. That's what hurt most of all.

While she didn't know Vince well, there were truths about him that she couldn't deny. He cared about his work, he cared about the man who'd been killed. The way she cared about exposing the evil that threatened her world.

It wasn't fair. None of it. All she wanted was to go back in time, to never have discovered anything about Omicron. She wanted that happy oblivion, because this was too hard. Nate and Seth, they were trained to fight, but she was just an optimistic fool who'd believed that people were basically good, and that she could make a difference. What a joke.

She sniffed and reached for some tissues. At least she'd stopped those gut-wrenching sobs. There was even some juice left, which cooled her aching throat. It was early, but still dark, and she couldn't exactly get up and go to the kitchen. Or turn on the television. Or disappear before she had to face Vince again.

She sat up in the strange bed, in the dark, in yet another room that wasn't hers. She thought about how she was going to leave Vince without so much as a goodbye, and, once gone, she'd never see him again. And when the tears reappeared, she let them fall. At least they were honest tears.

HER CELL PHONE WOKE HER. Disoriented, she had trouble finding it in her purse, and by the time she pressed the right button, the ringing had stopped. Nate. She rubbed her eyes and took another drink of juice, then called him back. He answered immediately.

"We've got trouble."

Not words she wanted to hear. "What?"

"They know you're in L.A. They have your picture and your name."

Her head dropped and her throat tightened. "Do they know where I am?"

"I don't know, but I'm sure they will soon enough."

"So?"

"I've talked to Cade and he's gonna take you in. We need one more day to get the transportation together. We should be ready to go by tomorrow night."

"And if they come for me before then?"

"You've got a cop and a gun. For the moment, that's gonna have to do."

"I don't want Vince getting killed over this."

Nate didn't say anything for a long minute. "It's the best I have, Kate. I'm sorry."

"Not your fault. Just, if you can do this faster, that would be good."

"Roger that. You be careful."

"I always am. What's going on with you guys?"

"Lots. We'll tell you all about it when we spring you."

"Tomorrow night," she said.

Nate disconnected. It was something that had taken getting used to—these soldier boys who didn't bother with goodbyes. Maybe that was the way to go.

She put her phone in the charger and headed for the

bathroom. When had she fallen asleep? It had been past four, that much she knew. She felt as though she hadn't slept but for five minutes. Her body ached, and she didn't even want to know how swollen her eyes were.

Whoa, they were worse than she'd guessed. Red, puffy, she looked like a woman who'd cried all night. Go figure.

She washed, hoping that would help, but nothing would, except time. There was no use worrying about it. It really didn't matter if Vince suspected. She was out of here tomorrow night, and that was going to be that.

She peeked in on him, still sleeping, stretched out on the big couch with only half a blanket covering him. He'd worn his jeans to bed, which didn't seem the most comfortable nightwear. His gun was on the floor, an inch from his hand.

Hers was under her mattress, which had been good last night, considering, but wouldn't be good enough today. If Omicron had recognized her, it wouldn't take them long to find her. Not with their connections.

She remembered what they'd done to Christie. For the unforgivable crime of being Nate's sister, they'd set her up, made her believe she was being stalked. She'd lost her job, her friends, and almost her life. Somehow, they'd even managed to get to the IRS. Christie's assets had been seized and she'd been left with nothing.

None of the team had any idea how they'd gotten so high up in the food chain, but the setup had reinforced Nate's position that he had to find out who was in charge of Omicron. It had to be someone in the government. Someone big. But so far, they'd had no luck getting a name or even an agency. Of course, Omicron was involved with the CIA, but what Omicron had done was so outside the CIA's purview, that there had to be madmen in charge.

Finding her at Vince's mother's house seemed like small potatoes. She knew without a doubt that Omicron would think nothing of killing Vince. They were completely ruthless. She hadn't lied to Vince about that recurring nightmare. Who knew where it had come from, but she'd always been absolutely terrified of being tortured. She knew she'd fold like a cheap paper bag, and how would she survive knowing she'd betrayed her friends?

It was too much. She was trembling and picturing all kinds of horrors, and that had to stop. She needed something to take her mind off Omicron.

She went back to the bedroom and got dressed. After putting her weapon in her purse, she took that to the kitchen and started the coffee. Making a big breakfast seemed an excellent way to keep busy, so she got out eggs, bacon, potatoes and bread. She'd never actually made hash browns from scratch, but it couldn't be that hard.

After going through the cupboards, she found an old box grater. That would keep her occupied for a while.

VINCE WOKE TO THE MOST amazing smells. Bacon, for sure, but there was something else in the mix, not counting coffee.

He stretched, then headed to the bathroom with a change of clothes. After a quick shower, he went straight to the kitchen, where the smells were even more intoxicating. "What's all this?"

"How do you like your eggs?"

"Over-medium," he said. "Can I help?"

"Nope." Kate was at the stove watching over a big

skillet full of hash browns. He didn't see the bacon, so it must be in the oven. She cracked a couple of eggs in the frying pan. What she didn't do was look at him.

His first reaction had been to kiss her. To touch that lovely neck, but no. Even someone as clueless as he was could see the Do Not Disturb sign. So he got some coffee and sat down at the table.

She didn't look up until she came to the table with his plate. Eggs, perfectly cooked, four slices of bacon, the potatoes and two slices of buttered toast. "Wow, what brought this on?"

She shrugged, still not meeting his eye.

"It looks great."

A small, tight smile was all he got in response, then she was back at the stove.

He'd seen enough, though. Her eyes looked worse for the long night, and her skin seemed pale and drawn. Something was tearing her up. As he ate, he thought about how to get her to talk. He didn't want to see her upset, but he wasn't about to forget about Tim just because they'd had sex.

He put his fork down as he remembered the feel of her. There was nothing, not in the whole world, that felt like being inside a woman. And to have that woman be responsive and vocal, and to feel her squeeze him as she got closer and closer to coming. That was home. That was heaven.

Shit, now he was getting hard again, and the last thing that was gonna happen in this house was a repeat performance. There probably shouldn't have been a first run, either. Clearly, she was sorry she'd done it. That didn't exactly make him feel like the man of the month. He wanted to ask her why, what had happened, but that question was even harder than asking her if she was an undercover agent.

She sat down at the other side of the table, and he watched her as she nibbled on the food. Mostly, she just moved it around. The clock on the mantel ticked loudly, and the sound of his fork on the plate clinked, but she was silent, withdrawn and still; she hardly ate a thing.

"Hey," he said, keeping his voice low. "You want to talk about it?"

She looked up at him, startled. "About what?"

"Nothing. Never mind."

He kind of expected her to press the issue. Most women he knew couldn't stand the "never mind" thing. But she just went back to playing with her food.

Finally, it was him that couldn't take it. "Did I do something wrong?"

"What? No." The way she said it made him believe her.

"So you're not sorry we…?"

She put her fork down, and for the first time that morning she looked right at him. "I'm only sorry we're in this wretched situation. I think you're a very decent guy. Someone I would have liked to get to know."

"I'm right here."

"No, you're not. You're not here with me, not really. You want me to give you something I can't. I was the one who started things. And while it was really great, I had my own reasons for taking you to my bed. Let's not pretend that we're lovers, okay, because that would make me feel terrible."

He wanted to argue with her. At least ask her what her reasons were, but he couldn't. He'd had his reasons, too. What she didn't know was that his plan hadn't worked in all sorts of ways. She hadn't told him what he wanted to know. And he hadn't expected to feel... Shit, he liked her. Even this, her unflinching honesty, made him want more. Of what, he wasn't sure.

She laughed, although it was rueful and sad. "You're not even going to argue?"

"Nope. I have to confess, I was kind of hoping you'd see what an honest, terrific guy I was and come clean about the whole shooting thing. Remember when I told you I could be a real moron?"

She gave him a smile that made him want to tell her all his secrets. "The truth is..." He shook his head. "I don't know if I can make you understand how important it is for me to get these guys."

"Oh, I understand. I wish you could believe that."

"See, that's what's making me crazy. I think you want to tell me. I think you're fairly bursting with it. But something big is holding you back, and I think I know what that is."

"You do, huh?"

"I think you're undercover. And I think you're working on something major, and that your life depends on your cover. But listen, if you are, then we can work something out. The courts, they understand about this stuff. They can take your testimony without revealing your identity."

"Stop," she said, and he heard that he'd pushed a very major button. "You're wrong. Let it go."

"Only I'm not wrong."

"Vince, listen to me. My heart breaks that I can't help you. But I cannot help you." She said it with such conviction that he almost believed her. Would have, if the stakes hadn't been so high.

"Okay, fine. You can't help me. But you're still stuck here, and screw it, I'm still gonna hope you change your mind. There isn't a damn thing we can do but wait while that gang is after you. So, if you're not going to talk to me, you might as well help me pack up my mother's crap."

She looked so exasperated that he almost smiled. But he didn't. He just got up and carried his plate to the sink. A few minutes later, she was beside him with her dishes. They got the work done silently, and that was okay. He still had time. He hoped that she would tell him the truth. Not just about what she'd seen in the hotel suite, but about why she'd cried such hard, hard tears. He'd really like to understand. And, God knew why, he'd like to help.

SETH HAD BROUGHT OVER some of the tranquilizer they'd used on a number of occasions, a gift of sorts from Harper. She hated it when any of them asked for her help, mostly because she was afraid she'd get her clinic in trouble. But she was a doctor, and she could get them stuff no one else could.

Nate liked Harper, and he felt bad that she was part of all this. Hell, he was sorry any of it had happened. But the one member of the team who kept him up nights was Tamara.

She didn't look like a scientist. She looked like a grad student, someone in the English department studying Emily Dickinson. But inside that little brain of hers was the one thing that could destroy all of Omicron's work.

Tamara had been recruited to work in the Balkans back in 2000. Of course, then she'd really been a grad student. She'd been lied to, and the idiots at Omicron had underestimated her. Their bad luck. Because when the team had gotten Tam out, she'd brought the key to their destruction with her. An antidote. In those last weeks just before the escape, she'd gotten her hands on the complete chemical makeup of the gas, and the work two of her colleagues had done on an antidote. She'd been working tirelessly since their return on testing the antidote, and coming up with a practical dispersal system.

The antidote would lessen the value of Omicron's precious weapon considerably once Tam put the pieces all together. He wished things would move more quickly, but she was one woman, and the task was huge. Now that he knew that Omicron was stockpiling the gas, there was even more urgency. Not that he'd tell Tam. All he could do for her was keep her safe, keep her focused, keep her sane, to the best of his ability. None of which was easy.

Ideally, when they discovered who was really in charge of Omicron and they had the proof they needed, Tam would come forward. And Omicron's precious weapon would be rendered obsolete before it could kill a single soul. *If* they could get the information they needed. *If* Omicron still believed the six of them remained a viable threat. *If...*

But for now, as always, Nate had to put one foot in front of the other. First, get Kate out of the state. Second, find out the exact location of the storage facility, then figure out what to do about it. Third, get some goddamn sleep so he could continue to function.

Seth had a connection to a car they'd use to get Kate out of town. It had plates that couldn't be traced, and if she was stopped somewhere between L.A. and Colorado Springs, nothing would tip the police off. She'd be Kate Hogan by then. Going on vacation to visit her brother.

"Nate, listen up."

He looked at Seth, who'd clearly been talking for a while, but he hadn't heard a word. "Go ahead."

Seth shook his head. "No, man. There's no way I'm taking you with me. I'll go see about the car myself."

"Don't be ridiculous."

"You're a liability, you got that? You need some sleep. All I have to do is give the man the documents. There's no reason you need to come along."

Seth was right. He couldn't put the sleep off any longer. He'd end up getting them all killed. "All right. I'll leave the phone on."

"Great." Seth stood up, checked his briefcase, then headed toward the door. "Do not go online. Is that understood?"

Nate saluted. Then he stretched out on his small bed. He didn't hear the door close.

SHE WATCHED VINCE as he grabbed all the books from the top shelf of the case and dropped them in a pile in a box. Kate shook her head in bafflement. If he wanted to throw the books away, he'd use a garbage bag. If he wanted to do something more productive with them, he was being a total idiot about it. "Where are those going?"

Vince jerked around, and she saw his hand went to

where his weapon would be holstered in an automatic reaction to being startled. He recovered quickly. "I don't know. Goodwill, I think."

"Then don't you think you should be a bit neater about boxing them up?"

"She's got a billion books up here."

"It's not quite that bad," Kate said, leaving her spot in the hall to join him in the living room. "Why don't you hand them to me, and I'll put them away."

"Fine with me, as long as you don't take forever. I want to clear this place out, and I swear she never threw a damn thing away her whole life."

"It'll go fast enough." She dumped the contents of the box on the floor, and gathered them together in a semblance of order. They were mostly paperback romances, but there were some hardcovers there, too. Some she'd love to take for herself, if she'd had a place to keep them. She missed books. She missed music, too. There was so much she'd left behind.

"Ready?"

She looked up. Vince, wearing a black T-shirt and jeans, looked very tall and imposing, standing on the ladder. The bookshelves were tall, all the way to the ceiling. "Did you build these shelves?"

"Yeah. I'm not a very good carpenter."

"No, they're great."

"Well, she never wanted to part with her stories. She called them keepers, and given half a chance she'd tell you the whole book in one sitting."

"I understand. I had a considerable keeper shelf myself."

"Not anymore though, huh?"

"No. Not anymore." She thought he was going to press, but he just handed her another stack of books. She put them away, thinking about the woman who'd loved them. When she took the next pile, she asked, "You don't read?"

"Sure I do. But I don't have an unnatural attachment to the damn books."

"You've never read anything twice?"

"No. What's the point? I already know what happens."

She smiled. She'd heard of people like Vince, but she wasn't one of them. Revisiting beloved books was one of her favorite things in the world. It didn't matter how many times she'd read *Pride and Prejudice,* she still thrilled at that first kiss, wept when Elizabeth finally realized that Mr. Darcy loved her truly and beyond measure.

"What's that sigh about?"

She grinned again. "Nothing you'd understand."

"Fine," he said. "Don't tell me."

He bent to give her more paperbacks, when something slipped from inside a book. She picked it up and found it was a picture of a young Vince, standing with a nice looking black man. They were both smiling over a trophy. "What's this?"

He looked at the photo, and his face changed. Softened. He climbed down and took it from her. "A guy I used to know."

"Someone important."

Vince nodded. "He's the reason I became a cop."

"Following in his footsteps?"

"Nah. He was an ex-junkie. He'd spent about thirty years behind bars."

"How did you meet him?"

"He shared a cell with my father."

9

VINCE LOOKED ONCE MORE at the picture of Jessie. Sometimes he missed the old man with a vengeance. Unlike his father, Jessie had written to him every week after that first time they'd met. He'd encouraged him to keep up his grades, to try to excel at everything he did. But mostly he'd kept hammering home that Vince wasn't destined to become a man like his father.

"Is your father still alive?" Kate asked.

"Nope. He died in jail three years ago. No one was particularly sorry to see him go."

"That must have been very difficult for you and your mother."

"We did okay. My old man, he had a mean streak in him. He was better at using his fists than most people were, and there weren't many who cared to go up against him."

"He hit you?"

"Hell, yeah. All the time. It was a relief when they sent him up that last time."

"How did he feel about you becoming a cop?"

"Pissed. Then he asked if I could get him a deal. Crazy sonofabitch."

"So your mother raised you by herself."

"She and Jessie, but I didn't see him all that often. Hell, I got into college, I joined the force. I have no regrets."

"Except that now you're quitting."

"I've done my time." He climbed back on the ladder, but only after putting the picture on the mantel. He had an old frame at his apartment that was just the right size. "What about you? Any jailbirds? Heroin addicts?"

She laughed. "Nope, sorry. Do-gooders from the word go."

"Oh?"

"My father's a lawyer for the ACLU. My mother works for the American Cancer Society."

"Holy crap. What did they want you to be? Glinda the Good Witch?"

"Something like that."

He heard the shift in her tone that told him she'd realized they'd gotten a little too close to the bone. "But you did go to college."

"Yep. Graduated, too. But I'm not going to tell you where."

"Why, you think I want to look up your transcripts?"

"I wouldn't put it past you."

"Kate, you wound me to the quick."

"I just call 'em like I see 'em."

"Fair enough." He finished clearing the top shelf and wondered if he was supposed to dust or something. Screw it. A potential buyer would have to climb up here to see the shelf, and if they were that anal they didn't deserve this house anyway.

As he started on the second shelf, it occurred to him that he'd had no hesitation telling Kate about his father. Mostly, he didn't talk about his childhood. Odd. But maybe not. Maybe it was easy to tell her because he knew she'd be gone, out of his life, one way or another. Which was a damn shame. He really liked her, despite everything.

"Will you miss it?" she asked.

"What?"

"Being a detective. It clearly means a lot to you."

"Past tense. It did."

"What changed?"

"I probably should have gotten out of the gang unit a long time ago. It's the toughest detail of all. Worse than homicide. It's all so senseless. So many kids killing each other."

"Tell me about Tim," she said.

He took in a deep breath before he handed her another stack of books. "He was a lot like Jessie, only without the heroin. Tim grew up in downtown L.A. His mother was a strawberry. You know what that is?"

"A crack addict who prostitutes for drugs, right?"

"Yep. He never knew who his father was. He was born addicted, but the county didn't take him away from his mother. Somehow he made it all the way through high school. He was in a gang, too."

"How did he get out?"

"All his friends were killed. Every last one. So he made up his mind to stop. To help other kids stop. It wasn't easy."

"I can imagine."

"No," he said, leaning on the ladder. "I don't think you can."

Kate stood and looked up at him. "He must have been an exceptional man."

Vince nodded. "One of the best. He risked his life every day. Lived below the poverty line just so he could keep working with these kids. He raised hundreds of thousands of dollars, but every penny went into Purchase House. You should have seen him work a room. It was something to behold."

She smiled, and when she did that her whole face lit up. All the puffiness from her crying jag had gone, leaving her as fresh and pretty as the day he'd first seen her. He felt a stirring inside, the want of her just under his skin.

"So you met him on the job?"

"Yep. He came to me when I'd arrested one of his kids. Not his own child, I mean one of the kids he looked after."

"What had he done?"

"Broken into a grocery store. I figured it was for drug money, but Tim convinced me that it wasn't that way. The kid needed money for medicine for his sister. I checked it out and found out he was telling the truth. We worked something out."

"What's going to happen to his kids now?"

"I don't know." He climbed down and wiped his hands on his T-shirt. "I have to make a phone call. Why don't we take a break."

"Sure," she said, looking at him carefully. "Whatever you want."

He left her in the living room while he went to the kitchen. After pouring himself another cup of coffee, he got out his cell and called Jeff.

"What's happening, my man?"

Jeff didn't respond immediately, which could mean the Captain was in range, or that there was bad news. Vince hoped for the former.

"Baker's been here."

"Oh?"

"He's pressing the lawsuit. He wants you gone, Vince, and he's really sticking it to Emerson."

Vince took a sip of coffee. "I don't care about that. What's going on with the investigation?"

"You don't... Vince, I'm not kidding. The Captain might not have any choice about this."

"It's okay, don't sweat it. Now come on. Has there been any progress on the case?"

"No. Nothing. No one's talking. They're too busy killing each other. It's bad out there, buddy. And there's a lot of collateral damage."

"Shit. I figured someone would have taken credit for the murder by now."

"There's more," Jeff said, lowering his voice.

"What?"

"You know that crap he was saying about Tim? About the drug connection?"

"Yeah. Total bullshit."

"I know, but Baker claims he's got evidence."

"What kind of evidence?"

"I don't know. He's not saying. The story is supposed to run, starting on Friday."

Vince cursed, visions of strangling Baker with his own microphone cord swimming in his head. "Aren't you friends with that copy editor at the *Times*?"

"Friends? I wouldn't go that far."

"See what you can dig up there, will ya? I need to know what that prick thinks he's got on Tim. Before the story runs."

"I'll try. Any luck with your lady?"

"Nope. She's a hard nut to crack. I'm not through trying yet, though."

"Good luck. And keep in touch, huh?"

"Will do."

He hung up, his thoughts on Baker and his insane idea about Tim. The man had despised drugs. The reporter was so off base that it was worrisome. Someone was giving him bad intel, but why? Who would stand to gain if Tim's legacy were destroyed? It just didn't make sense. His murder—that at least made some horrible sense. Without Tim, the gangs were in charge, and no one in their hood got gone. It was a control issue. And gangs were nothing if not about control.

But to paint Tim as a drug dealer, now that was perverse. It made Vince sick to his stomach, and it gave him a whole new agenda: find out who killed Tim first, then find out who was behind these lies. And if Baker happened to get humiliated, or even, say, fired in the process, so much the better.

KATE CLOSED THE DOOR to the small bedroom and dumped the fresh sheets on the dresser. It felt good to strip the bed. She'd have preferred going for a run, but she'd take what she could get.

She'd been so tempted to take one of those books. Oh, man, to curl up in a big, comfy chair with some tea and cookies and a thick historical novel. She sighed and punched the pillow before she put the case on. She thought about the ledgers waiting for her, but they would have to wait until she was at Cade's.

She put on the clean sheets, then the comforter, and gathered the dirty sheets for the washer. But as she headed for the door, her throat tightened again. Tears were right there, a blink away, and it was crazy because there was nothing wrong. All she had to do was wait for tomorrow night, and all this would be over. She'd be on her way to Colorado, where no one knew her. She wouldn't have to worry about testifying or hurting Vince. He'd go on and find those Asian killers, she felt sure he would. And then...

And then. She'd still be living a lie. She still wouldn't be able to talk to her mother. Or go to a club or on a date.

She sat down on the edge of the bed and dropped the sheets. Her energy drained, all she wanted to do was lie down, go to sleep and wake up when the world made sense again. Nothing was fair or right. The bad guys won all the time, and the good guys got mowed down in hotel rooms by teenagers with no hope. The only good thing that had happened to her in such a long time was that she'd been able to escape, for a little while at least, last night.

She ran her hand over the faded flower bedspread, then put her head down on the nearest pillow. She took the other one and pulled it to her chest, hugging it tight.

The truth was, she liked Vince. A lot. More than anyone she'd met in a long, long time. If things had been different, she'd have pursued a relationship with him. Although she didn't quite believe he was going to give up police work, she would have liked to see what he'd do next. He was a good man, with good priorities, and the way he'd made love to her...

She rocked on the bed, willing herself not to cry. She shouldn't have tears. They didn't do anybody a damn bit of good. She'd learned that from her soldiers, among other lessons. Like not leaving anything behind. Like keeping herself separate.

It hadn't been smart, telling Vince about her folks. She should have just stayed in the bedroom until her escape. But it was so against her nature.

Back in her life, she'd been a very outgoing person. She loved meeting new people, learning about different cultures. Kosovo had been a fascinating experience for her, and she'd developed a deep affection for the people she'd met there. She wanted to tell Vince about it. Hell, she wanted to tell him about everything. If he wasn't so very determined to get her testimony, she might have. But it was clear that he'd never see that her silence was just as important as getting Tim's killers.

With her eyes closed and the softness of the pillow in her arms she turned her thoughts from the overwhelming sadness of it all to the little spots of light. Like being able to cook with fresh ingredients on a decent stove. Like sleeping in a warm bed. Or not sleeping at all.

He was right up there with the best kissers on the planet. No, she hadn't tried all the men, but she'd kissed her fair share, and Vince was definitely number one. Funny, back home, before she'd gone overseas, she'd never have dreamed of sleeping with a guy unless they were serious. But then her whole life had become serious as hell, and, while she didn't give it away, she'd taken comfort where she could. Also funny, but the others, and there'd been only three including Nate, hadn't affected her like this. There'd been no regrets at all. But she was sorry she'd slept with Vince. Sorry she'd listened to his stories. Sorry for the whole damn mess.

She needed to forget his touch, his kiss, the way he'd run his hands over her body. It would just make her angry and then she'd start crying, which simply wouldn't do.

Instead she should focus on her job. Without the paper trail, it would be very difficult to convict the bastards, and, like Vince, she was all about putting the pricks behind bars. Damn it.

She sat up, tossing the pillow to the head of the bed. Vince wasn't such a goddamned special guy. He was simply there. That was it. She'd been cut off from normal interactions for too long, which made him appear to be Mr. Wonderful, when, in fact, he was just a cop. A relentless cop who'd do anything he had to, to get the information he needed.

He hadn't denied that he'd slept with her to get her to talk, right? So why wasn't she pissed about that? He'd used her. Okay, she'd used him, too, but that wasn't the point. She'd only known him a few days, so how could she even think she liked him?

She picked up the dirty sheets once more and headed to the laundry room. Vince was back at the bookshelf, but she wasn't going to go there. What did she care how he packed? She'd be gone tomorrow.

Colorado was nice. She'd been there once as a kid, and it had been so beautiful. And, though she didn't know Cade well, he was a pleasant enough guy. A sharpshooter. Talk about feeling safe.

Yeah, Colorado would be perfect. She'd find herself an innocuous job, and at night she'd whip through those ledgers. She'd been trained well, so she knew she could put together an ironclad case as long as all the paperwork was there. If it wasn't, at least she'd know what to ask for when she contacted Branislav again.

She poured the detergent and the powdered bleach, then put the sheets in the washer. It was an old machine, but she wasn't in a laundromat and it wasn't the middle of the night, and she didn't have to keep looking out the window, terrified that she'd be shot and left to die on some filthy floor. Oh, yeah, she was livin' large.

"What's so funny?"

She whipped around, startled at Vince's voice. "What?"

"You were laughing."

"No, I wasn't."

"I heard you."

"Well, it was nothing."

He seemed skeptical. "If you'd called me, I would have helped with the bed."

The washer kicked on. "I can change sheets," she said. The room was too small for him to be so close. She folded her arms over her chest, wishing he'd go back to packing.

He smiled at her, but it wasn't a regular smile. This was more the way a person would smile at a nutcase, to make them not go off the deep end. "You all right?"

"I'm fine. Just tired, that's all."

He nodded. "I kept you up pretty late last night. I'm sorry."

"No need to apologize. I'm a big girl. I could have kicked you out anytime."

"Yeah," he said slowly. "You could have. Are you sure nothing's wrong?"

"Don't you have to pack? Because I have things to do, too. Like look for a job."

"We don't have a newspaper."

"I brought my own."

"Ah. Okay then. I don't want to interrupt the job search."

He might have said he didn't want to interrupt, but he didn't back off. Standing in the middle of the door like that? He was trying to start something, she just knew it. And where was her training? She didn't get flustered. Not anymore. She was tough and cool, and, dammit, she knew hand-to-hand.

"Kate?"

She jerked again, which pissed her off even more. Rather than answering him, she decided to leave. Go to the bedroom and lock the door. It was the only solution.

Only, he didn't move. Not when she was right in front of him, and not when she tried to pass. What he did instead was touch her arm. One hand, gently laid.

The second it happened, she burst into tears. Totally without warning, completely without provocation. Big sobs, giant tears, legs wobbly, hands trembling, it was all she could do not to slide down on the linoleum in a giant puddle.

In fact, she would have, but Vince pulled her into his arms and held on tight. She leaned on him and tucked her head into the curve of his neck and wept like a baby. It was worse than last night because he was right there, watching, rocking her, whispering, "Shh, it's okay," but it wasn't okay. She didn't even know why she was having this meltdown, why it felt so necessary to hang on to him, to feel his hard body. Or why she couldn't stop.

She hurt in every kind of way. And the sobbing went on and on—and loud, even with the washing machine going. He rubbed her back, but that didn't stop her either, so she tried to break away, only he wouldn't let go.

He said her name, over and over, but she couldn't open her eyes. She didn't want to see him, she didn't want him to see her, and she struggled, but even that didn't get him to ease his grip.

It was only when he kissed her, when his lips pressed hers hard, when his tongue slipped inside her, when his palm went to the back of her head, that she stopped.

She wasn't sure if this was worse, though. Holding on to him so tightly she knew he'd have bruises. Kissing him back with a desperation that was completely pathetic. Praying that he'd take her back to the little bedroom and make love to her until the whole universe disappeared.

10

VINCE PULLED BACK, not because he wanted to but because he had to. The need he had for her was at odds with what he needed her for, and that wasn't good at all. Her pain cut his thinking to shreds so that all that mattered was to take away the hurt. "Who did this to you?" he whispered. "What happened?"

She shook her head, then broke free with a jerk. She started out of the room, but he couldn't let her go—he grabbed her again, and she spun around, shoved him away, then tried another escape.

"Wait," he said, sorry as hell he'd spoken at all. "Wait, don't leave. Don't go."

She'd made it halfway through the kitchen, but her step faltered and finally she stopped. Not turning, she leaned heavily on the counter as if she was going to pass out.

He put his arm around her waist. "Come on," he said, keeping his voice low, afraid to spook her. "It's okay."

"No, it's not," she said. She was still weeping, but quietly now, the tears dripping down her cheeks. "Nothing's okay. It's all gone to hell."

"I won't let you fall," he said, walking her out of the kitchen and down the hall. She was tall and despite the strength he'd seen in her from the first, she felt frail, tiny. So beaten up. By what? The only time he'd seen this before was from victims of assault. Post-traumatic stress? Maybe. He didn't think it was because she'd seen Tim get killed, although he wouldn't completely rule that out. The only thing he knew for sure was that she needed help. He was just the last person in the world who should try to offer it.

When they got to the bedroom, he threw the covers back and helped her into bed. She put up no struggle. Not even when he took off her shoes, and pulled the blankets over her. All she did was turn over and curl up on herself.

This wasn't good. He felt helpless, and he hated that, but what was he supposed to say? Without words, he went around the bed, kicked off his own shoes, and climbed in next to her. She didn't move. Not to welcome him or push him away.

When he touched her shoulder, he felt her tremble. "Kate?"

She sniffed, but said nothing.

The only thing he could safely offer her was comfort. So he moved closer and wrapped his arm around her. She shifted so that her body pressed against his, so her head was in the crook of his neck.

He rubbed her back in big, lazy circles. Slowly, she relaxed, and just when he thought she was asleep, he felt her hand on his T-shirt, pulling it out of his jeans.

He wasn't at all sure this was a good idea. But he was even less sure that he should stop her. That he wanted to stop her.

She lifted her head, and her soft lips touched the side of his face. She kissed him as if she wasn't sure, although her hands had no doubts. His shirt free, she managed to undo the buttons of his jeans, and when they were undone she reached into his shorts to grasp his penis.

He gasped and arched and she followed him when he fell on his back. A tear fell on his cheek as she kissed him again, hard. Determined.

He groaned as she pumped his already hard cock, as her tongue skimmed his teeth then plunged deep into his mouth. One last vestige of sanity remained, and he used that to hold her arms still and pull his head away.

"Vince," she said, breathless and confused.

"Slow down, Kate."

"Why?"

"Because I need you to."

She blinked at him. Her eyes were puffy again, and red-rimmed. She frowned, but he was still watching her eyes, knowing he'd see the truth there.

Kate sat up, pulling her hand out of his pants. Her head spun from tears she didn't understand and the physical need that coursed through her whole body. What was her deal? Was she completely losing her mind?

The only thing that made sense was to escape. To fall into the only safe thing she could find. Looking at him, knowing he was hard and ready, but that he'd put on the brakes anyway, made her more sure than ever. Whatever else he wanted from her, he also wanted *her*. He hadn't lied, he wasn't playing games. This was who he was, and for right now she could be herself. Not Katherine Ashman, because that girl had disappeared in Kosovo, but Kate. Different last names be damned, she was Kate and she needed to be held and kissed and loved, even if it was just for the moment. All she had were moments, most of them so scary she could hardly breathe. But not this one.

"I want this," she said. "If you do."

He looked at her for a while, looked right into her eyes, and then he smiled. It was a little naughty, but mostly it was kind and welcoming. He pulled her back down, right into a kiss that made everything better.

He took the lead, which was fine with her. Rolling her over, he undressed her slowly. Sweet man, he teased and touched her with his skillful hands, making a fuss over her poor, plain underwear. When she was naked, he gave her a little show when he stood up on the bed to remove his jeans. There was a breathless minute when he almost fell, but a well-placed foot saved the day.

His eagerness hadn't flagged at all. Or maybe it was just that she was more relaxed. The room seemed warmer, the world farther away as he kissed her belly, licking her skin, twining his fingers with hers. Until, that is, he found a better way to use them.

He urged her to spread her legs with his head. He nudged her inner thigh until he had her just where he wanted her. Then, with a rhythm she didn't understand, he licked her, tickled her, dipped inside her to rub in that perfect way. With closed eyes and a total willingness to be led wherever he cared to take her, she moaned her pleasure. Lifted her hips to signal her delight.

When he pulled away, she was very mature and hardly pouted at all. Because she trusted him. God, what a miracle to trust someone.

"Kate?"

"Hmm?"

"Turn over."

"What?"

He kissed the hollow of her neck. "Come on, do it."

"Why?"

"Don't think, just turn."

Hadn't she just said she trusted this man? She opened her eyes, just to check, and yes, his eyes still looked kind. If just a little naughtier.

She turned over, slowly, then hugged the pillow wondering what he had in mind. She didn't have to wait long.

His hands, broad and warm and surprisingly talented, went to work, starting with her neck. He massaged every muscle, some she hadn't even realized were tense. She lost track of time, of everything except for the feel of his kneading palms. Well, not everything. He hummed.

It was a tune she didn't recognize, but it was hypnotically soft and wonderfully dreamy. By the time he hit her lower back, she was goo.

"Kate?"

"Hmm?"

He continued to work his wonders as he whispered, "Do you know what I am?"

"What?" she said, although she doubted he could understand her as her mouth was pressed into the pillow.

"I'm a detective. I live to uncover mysteries. And you... I don't know the first thing about you."

She stiffened. Please, not now. Not when she was so happy.

"Don't worry," he said. "This isn't an interrogation. But there's something you need to know."

His hand ran up her spine so softly she shivered. "I don't suppose that I'll ever get my answers," he said, and he was closer, leaning over her. His lips came still closer to her ear. "But here's the weird part. I don't think I give a damn."

She breathed out, a sigh of gratitude and thanks. She couldn't stay on her stomach a moment longer. Turning over, she opened her arms, and he came to her. For a while, they didn't do anything but hug. With their bodies touching all the way down. Him so hard and big, and safe and safe and safe.

When she moved, it was in invitation. She pulled him close with her legs, centered him with a shift of her hips. He entered her with the same patience he'd used on her muscles. In this, there was no mystery. None at all.

SHE FOUND HERSELF HUMMING the tune while she was in the kitchen. She wasn't making anything special—tuna fish salad, but with grapes and walnuts. She wished the knife was better, but it did feel good in her hand. It was an easy kitchen to work in. Small, tidy. And it was really nice to make a meal for someone she cared about.

Yes, she knew that it was over tomorrow, but she didn't care. Tonight, she would enjoy whatever she could. Wallow in her feelings, let her imagination go. Not too far, because that would make her crazy, but she could think about the rest of the night. How they'd eat, and talk a little and maybe laugh. She hadn't laughed in a long time, and, like his massage, she knew it would do her wonders.

She went to the fridge and got out the bottle of white wine. What the hell, right? She debated bringing a glass to Vince, but he was probably still sleeping, and she guessed he needed it.

So she just poured herself a little and went on chopping and humming.

VINCE STARED AT THE CEILING, debating his next move. He should get up, find out what Kate was doing, grab a quick shower. But he couldn't stop thinking about what he'd seen. She'd really lost it, and while he liked to think having sex with him could cure anything, he wasn't quite that vain. She was in trouble, and it was bad.

He got out of bed and put on his jeans. When he opened the door, he heard her humming in the kitchen. She must be making food, which was a really good thing. He was starving. But…

He closed the door again, not at all sure he should be doing this. But, dammit, she needed someone's help, and it didn't appear that anyone else was raising his hand.

He went to the closet, and there was the box. From the first, he knew there was something important in it, something she would protect to the end. Whatever was going on in that beautiful head was connected to that damn box, and he needed to know what it contained. Maybe it was about a stalker, although he doubted it. There was something more, an immediate threat, and it was big.

He took off the top of the box, and there were papers, copies, and not good ones. Crouching down, he picked up a stack and saw they were financial books. Ledgers. Blurred numbers in columns. On the far left, he saw listed subjects. Transportation, fuel, emergency preparation, which was broken down into a number of other columns. All the pages were like the first. The subjects were strange, though, and when he looked at the top of the page he saw the logo for the United Nations.

What the hell?

Moving more quickly, he went down deeper into the box, but there was nothing but more of the same. He had no idea what the ledgers represented, or why Kate would have them. The U.N.? It made absolutely no sense.

He put the papers back, realizing it would take a hell of a lot longer than he had to figure this out. After covering the box, he closed the closet, then grabbed his shirt and his shoes.

He left the bedroom, thinking about what he'd seen, trying to get a handle on any part of it, when Kate came into the hallway with a smile that knocked him on his ass.

When was the last time anyone was so happy to see him? Jeez, he couldn't recall. She wore an oversized white T-shirt and her jeans, but her feet were bare, and he got that hitch inside that made him want to take her right back to bed. The knife in her hand dissuaded him, but at least he got a great kiss.

"Dinner's almost ready. You want to shower first?"

He nodded. "I could sure use somebody to wash my back."

She laughed. "Sorry, buddy. That's what you get for being so lazy."

"You're a cruel, cruel woman."

She kissed him again. "Go. Be clean."

"There's not enough water in the world."

With a flick of that glorious hair, she went back to the kitchen, and he watched her until she vanished behind the door.

He headed to the bathroom, but he heard his cell ringing in the living room. Hustling, he got it just before it switched to voice mail. "Yarrow."

"Vince."

It was Jeff. He didn't sound happy. "What now?"

"Hold on a sec."

Vince listened as Jeff told someone a file was already in the archives, then nothing for almost a full minute. He was about to hang up, when Jeff said, "It's Baker."

"Yeah?"

"That article in tomorrow's *Times?* The Captain got a copy, and he's fuming."

"What's it say?"

"That the department is conspiring against his suit by announcing your suspension, when they knew that you were holding the only witness to Tim's murder."

"Shit."

"Yep."

"Did he go into detail?"

"I don't know. I didn't see the whole thing, just the first paragraph. Emerson kicked me out when the brass called."

"Well, there's nothing I can do about it now." He walked into the bathroom and closed the door, not wanting Kate to overhear. She had enough to worry about. "Did Emerson say what he was going to do about it?"

"Other than fire your ass?"

"Yeah, other than that."

"Nope. But he wanted everything we had on Kate Rydell."

"Can you stall him?" Vince asked.

"I'll see what I can do, but, Vince, if he tells you to bring her in, you'd better. The mood he's in, he'll lock you both away."

"Right. Keep me informed, would ya?"

"Yeah. You gonna stay at your mom's place?"

"For tonight, at least."

"Okay. Stay safe."

"Thanks." He hung up, and started the shower. Things were going to get worse before they got a lot worse.

11

THE WIND PICKED UP outside, blustery and cold, but Kate felt warm all over as Vince finished up his dinner. He'd never had tuna with grapes before, and even though it was one of the simplest things she made, she felt inordinately pleased. The wine didn't hurt, either, but she stopped after one and a half glasses. She had no desire to be tipsy, not when she was having such a nice time right here.

She wouldn't let herself think about tomorrow, although she did steal thoughts of later on, when they went back to the bedroom. No tears, no angst, this time she would just enjoy him and how he made her tummy do flip-flops, among other things.

"She used to make German apple pancakes," Vince said, leaning back in his chair. "Man, they were good. Huge, too, with lots of honey butter on the side."

"It must have been nice to have a mother who knew how to cook."

"Yours didn't?"

"Not very well." Kate shook her head. "She didn't enjoy it, so she made a lot of frozen stuff. And chicken. Dried out chicken."

"So you became a cook in self-defense."

"Basically. I took some classes at an extension university. And I had some friends who showed me a thing or two."

"Where'd you learn this?" he nodded at the crumbs left over from the meal.

"A magazine. It's really nothing. I just wanted something simple tonight."

"Well, maybe tomorrow we can delve deeper into your repertoire."

She smiled and gave him a brief nod, not wanting to lie out loud. "You know what I'd like to do tonight?"

"What?"

"Watch a movie. I saw a whole bunch of DVDs in the living room. I haven't been to a movie in ages."

"Not a problem. Pick out anything you'd like."

Her smile was genuine as she got up to clear the table. Together, they finished the dishes in no time.

Vince touched her a lot, little brushes of his hand or his shoulder. A kiss to her neck, a palm on the small of her back. She reciprocated, although she felt shy about it, which didn't make a whole lot of sense. She wasn't a totally touchy-feely kind of person, but she appreciated what it meant to connect skin to skin. With Vince, though, maybe because she knew this was the last night, every gesture felt magnified. Just below her contentment there was that small buzz of anxiety that he'd figure out she was planning to leave, or that she'd let something slip that would put him in danger.

Thankfully, he didn't bring up Tim's name, not even once. She found a movie that had been hugely popular, one she could tell he'd seen before, but he didn't seem to mind a repeat viewing.

The only DVD player was in the living room, so they cuddled together on the couch. He had a beer, she had a cup of tea, and the movie was funny and sweet, but not half as wonderful as just being there. Leaning against his shoulder. Folding her hand in his. She felt normal. Well, as normal as she could.

When the movie ended, she excused herself. "Give me a bit," she said, leaning over to kiss his forehead. "I have girly things to do."

He grinned. "Half an hour's about all I can take."

"I'll be done." She headed to the bedroom, wishing like crazy that she had some sexy negligee to wear. Or any negligee, for that matter. Her clothes were not exactly the stuff dreams were made of. On the other hand, she probably wouldn't be wearing them for long.

So she got out her sleep shirt and her toiletries. There were parts to wash, to shave, to rub with lotion. All those things that were a chore without a totally delicious man in the living room.

She had it all together when she glanced at the closet. Her heart stood still as she saw the door ajar. Not much, but enough. She'd left it closed all the way.

Dropping her stuff on the bed, she pushed the sliding door open far enough for her to see the box. Her pulse raced and she hoped with all her heart she was wrong but she didn't even have to take off the lid to realize he'd been there. Her tell, the small piece of tape she put on the edge of the box, was now only connected to the box top. He hadn't noticed. But then, that was the point.

Seth had taught her this little trick, and she'd seen everyone on the team mark windows, doors, anything that shouldn't be disturbed with a marker, practically invisible to any intruder. Like Vince.

Oddly, she didn't cry this time. She just got pissed. Really, really pissed. And then, she got busy.

Five minutes later, she was packed. Luckily, information had a taxi company listed in Tujunga, and she'd memorized the address. She hung up, then dialed Nate.

He'd been sleeping, she could hear it in his voice.

"Sorry to bother you, but I need help."

"What happened?"

"I'll explain later. I'm not in danger, but I need to get out tonight, not tomorrow. Can you do it?"

"Yeah, sure. Where?"

"Not here. I've called a taxi. Do you have a place to meet?"

He was silent for a while, then he said, "Sunland. The corner of Sunland and Tuxford. I'll be there in about forty-five minutes."

"Great. It's a Yellow Cab." She hung up, and her heart sank with renewed sadness but she pushed it away. No more tears. She wouldn't cry about Vince. He was no one, nothing to her. They'd had sex, that's all. They'd both lied to each other to get what they wanted, period, the end. Too damn bad. Anything else was fantasy, and God knew, she couldn't afford to stand anywhere but squarely in reality.

She had no idea how long it would take for the taxi to get there, but she figured she'd wait outside, near the hedges, just in case.

The last thing she had to get was her gun, which she pulled out from under the mattress. She'd become so familiar with it that making sure it was ready to rock was like brushing her teeth. One could get used to anything, in time.

She put on her coat, put her gun in her pocket, then pulled the box out of the closet. It wasn't easy carrying everything at once, but she'd managed it before. With the box on top of the suitcase, she could still see, even though it was really heavy.

This, however, was the part she wished she could avoid. He'd have questions, excuses. It didn't matter. Damn him. Straight to hell.

She opened the bedroom door, then picked up her big bundle. Halfway down the hall, she heard his footsteps, and then he was standing between her and leaving.

"Kate? What's going on?"

"I have to go."

"What? Why?"

"It doesn't matter. I just have to go."

"It's too dangerous out there."

"Thank you for your concern, but I'll be fine."

He walked closer to her, and made as if to take the box. She jerked around, sorry she couldn't get to her gun. "Don't."

"Would you just stop a minute. What the hell's going on?"

"I already told you. You have no right to keep me here, so get out of my way."

"Kate."

"Do it."

He sighed, his eyes troubled and his hands curled in tight fists. "Look, I just wanted to help—"

"Get away from the door."

"I—"

"Goddammit," she said, her voice just under an outright scream. "Move."

He did. He went into the living room, where her tea was still on the coffee table, where the books she'd packed were stacked against the wall. She wouldn't look. Not at the kitchen or the bookcase or at him. She just went to the door, pressed her bundle against the wall so she could get to the knob, then she walked outside, not bothering to shut the door behind her.

The cab wasn't there yet, so she walked to the side of the house where she found a nice dark spot. There, she put her things down in front of her and she waited, her right hand in her pocket, holding the Glock.

He didn't come outside, but she knew he was watching. Not that she could see him, but of course he would. As he'd so recently reminded her, he was a detective. He had to uncover mysteries. She felt pretty damn sure he was going to follow her in the cab, too. But she also knew that Nate would lose him, and that they could replace the car's license plate when they got to his place. Try as he might, Vince would never find her. She was one mystery he'd never solve. And that was fine with her.

She swallowed hard and stopped the tears in their tracks. He'd violated her trust. There was no question about that, no shading she could give that would explain it away. He'd fucked her, then fucked her over.

The sad thing was, she wasn't surprised. Not really. It made some awful sense, given her life for the last few years. Betrayal seemed to be the central theme, with a soupçon of irony thrown in for color.

Why couldn't he have just left it alone? She would

have been gone tomorrow, and it would have been bitter-sweet, but okay. Not like this. This sucked. Sucked so bad.

THE CAB HAD TURNED on Sunland Boulevard, heading southwest. Vince had cursed himself for a fool for the last twenty minutes, but it didn't make him feel one iota better.

Goddammit, he'd been trying to help. Not that it mattered. He'd blown it, and he'd blown it so success-fully that there was no hope of getting her back. Emerson *should* fire him.

What he couldn't figure out was where she was going. He knew nothing of her life, nothing about her past, so all he could do was follow her and hope to get lucky. He'd take anything at this point.

The worst part of it was that he didn't just want her back because of Tim. The thought of never seeing her again was more unsettling than he cared to admit. He may have known her for only a few days, but something had clicked between them. He wasn't the kind to have had that happen very often.

The cab turned onto another long stretch of lonely road, heading, he guessed, toward Sunland. There wasn't much out here, not in this part of the city. Ranches, mostly, with only one restaurant, an occasional gas station. In the far distance there were more lights, but here it was dark and the wind had the sparse billboards swaying.

He had to keep his distance. Maybe she knew he was following, but, then again, she'd been so furious, she might not think it through. Doubtful, but he'd be careful nonetheless.

A car, a big boat of a Buick, pulled out of a dark side

street between him and Kate's cab. He switched lanes to pass, but the Buick picked up speed.

Not good. Pure cop's instinct had him jam his foot on the gas as the Buick raced up on the taxi. Then the guns came out.

A semiautomatic from the backseat—it was the goddamn gang. He could see the shooter's head, a black rag low down over the forehead. Crips, probably, but he was still too far back to see.

He got his gun out, pressed the safety off. Wished like hell he had a radio in this car.

The first shots hit the back of the cab, and he saw Kate go down. He didn't know if she'd ducked or if she'd been shot. He kept his foot on the pedal and held on tight as he rammed the Buick.

Gunshots sprayed the front of his car, blowing right through the windshield. A bullet screamed so close to his ear it singed his hair.

He aimed into the backseat, firing just before he rammed the Buick a second time. His head jerked back and his right shoulder burned as another bullet slammed into his seat.

The cab had stopped, front wheels over the sidewalk, and the driver's door swung open. Just as Vince was going to ram it again, more gunfire sprayed, only this time it was from the backseat of the cab. The Buick swerved crazily, then spun. He hit the back end of it, spinning both cars. He ended up next to the cab, while the Buick wrapped around a phone pole.

Vince jumped out of the car and ran toward Kate. Before he could get to her, another car came speeding down the road from the other direction.

Gunshots peppered the tar around his feet as he reached the back door of the cab. He jerked it open, terrified to see her lying in a pool of blood, but the way she was pointing a gun in his face told him she was all right. "It's me."

The gun dropped. "Get out of here," she shouted. "Leave."

"The hell I will," he said. He turned to face the Buick, crouching behind the cab's door. But the other car, the new one, drove in between the cab and the Buick, and someone jumped out of the passenger side, shooting into the Buick's windshield.

The driver got out, shouting, but Vince couldn't make out the words.

Who the hell were these guys? A rival gang? It didn't matter. He had to get Kate out of there. "Come on. Move." He reached for her, but she jerked back.

"Leave," she said again, and then she opened the other door, pulled the box behind her and got out. Her suitcase was between them, and he shoved it out of his way.

He ducked as the back window shattered, as gunfire slammed into the trunk like rain. Someone screamed, and it was the sound of death.

More gunfire, only this time, it didn't hit the cab. He sat up, looked back. There were three people on the ground, all from the Buick. As Vince watched, the last man stood and took aim. Before he could get him in his sights, the shooter was down, and the gunshot had come from the other side of the cab. Kate.

He turned to look at her, but she was already running toward the second car, the box in her hands.

Vince stood and headed after her, pulling his cell phone out to get some assistance. Only he didn't have a chance to dial. Another car, a goddamn Mercedes, came screaming down the road, heading right for Vince's car.

Where they'd come from, he didn't know, but they were not stopping, not even trying to hit the brakes. With a crash that made the ground shake, they rammed into his car, sending it careening into the back of the Buick. He ducked, covering his head, as one of the cars burst into flames. He looked for Kate, but he couldn't find her. Christ, she'd been right there. Right in front of the burning Buick.

KATE WOKE UP on the pavement, her head throbbing and the box overturned. Papers were scattering in the wind, illuminated by the flames that engulfed the car. She got up, the sounds of gunfire louder than the crackling of the fire.

As she grabbed papers and stuffed them back in the box, she heard sirens in the distance, which meant she, Nate and Seth had to get out of there, pronto. But she couldn't leave any pages behind. Even one could do them irreparable damage.

"Kate, goddammit, get out of there."

Vince stood over her, his sleeve bloody, his face quivering in the light of the blaze.

"Go away. You can't be here."

"Leave the damn—" He stopped, lifted his weapon and let go a round.

She ignored him and continued getting the ledger paper. She'd seen enough to know that the men who were trying to kill her weren't the Asian gang. It was Omicron, although she had no idea how they'd tracked her. And now she'd gotten Nate and Seth in the mix, not to mention Vince. His car was destroyed, he was shot, who knew how badly. Well, the police would get here soon enough, and he'd be fine. She'd be fine, too, if she could just get the rest of the papers in the box and get the hell out of there.

She looked behind her, past Vince, and saw that the body count had risen. But there were Nate and Seth, crouched behind the car doors, doing what they'd been trained to do.

Vince swore loudly, then he put his weapon in his waistband and joined her, gathering the papers. "The gas tank's going to blow any minute," he shouted. "I hope these pages are worth it."

"I don't need your help."

"The hell you don't."

She ran closer to the car to retrieve a page that was already singed. As soon as she had it, she felt a tug on her coat and she was pulled back. Vince shoved her away as he went perilously close to the fire. He got everything he could, then ran like hell back to where she waited. As far as she could see that was the end of it. She stuffed the pages inside the box and closed it.

"Can we get out of here now?"

"We aren't going anywhere. You're waiting for the police."

"Oh, no—"

An explosion knocked him into her, and they fell on the hard ground, his elbow jabbing her in the ribs, knocking the wind out of her. Of course, she'd landed right on her head again, and, for a moment, she thought she was going to lose it.

Behind her, she heard a bloodcurdling scream, and

her heart froze. Maybe she was disoriented, maybe the scream hadn't come from Nate's car.

She pushed Vince away and got to her hands and knees. As she watched, Nate shot the last of the men from the Mercedes, then he ran around the car. To Seth. On the ground.

She was on her feet a moment later, running. When she got to the men, Nate had dropped his jacket and was taking off his T-shirt. Seth was holding on to his left wrist. The hand above it was covered in blood, and there was a space where his thumb should have been.

She watched numbly as Nate swathed the terribly wounded hand, applying pressure. A moment later, Vince crouched down next to Nate. He had a belt in his hand, and he fashioned a tourniquet out of it.

Nate looked up at Kate. "Get the box. Put it in the trunk."

She obeyed, amazed that her feet worked, that she could follow the simple order. The sirens were getting closer, and that made her move even faster.

She put the box away, stunned at how many bullet holes had gone through the back of the car. When she turned, Nate and Vince were carrying a very still Seth into the backseat. Vince got in with him, holding the tourniquet tight.

Nate climbed behind the wheel. She went to the passenger side and the second she closed the door, Nate gunned it. They turned off the road before the police got there.

She wondered if Seth would be all right. If she'd gotten all the Kosovo papers. What the police would make of the carnage. And what the hell she was going to do with Vince.

12

"WHAT THE HELL'S GOING ON?" Nate whispered, although Kate was sure Vince could hear him.

"I'll explain later. Where are we going?"

"To Harper. Goddammit. What happened? How did they find you?"

"I have no idea."

"Uh, there's a hospital about a mile from here, if you get on the freeway," Vince suggested from the backseat.

She turned to look back at Vince. Seth was still unconscious, which was a good thing, and Vince had the wounded man's head cradled in his lap. He still had the belt tight at Seth's wrist, and she just hoped like hell Seth didn't die before they got to Harper's place.

"We're not going to a hospital," Nate said.

Vince cursed. "Who the hell are you?"

"That's none of your goddamn business."

"I'm a cop, you idiot."

"A suspended cop."

Kate looked at Nate, then back at Vince. "What?"

"He didn't tell you? He was suspended three days ago. I doubt very much he was supposed to be watching you. Or even have a gun."

"You didn't think that was necessary information?"

she asked, incredulous. "My God, did you lie about everything?"

"It wasn't important. As you saw so vividly tonight, a gang is out to kill you."

She almost spoke, but a glance from Nate made her turn away from Vince.

"If you don't get him to a hospital, he's going to lose the whole hand," Vince said.

"We're taking him to a doctor. Kate, get out my cell and press five, would you?"

"I hope he knows what he's doing," Vince said.

"*She* does." Nate turned on yet another dark, small street. If they let Omicron catch them now, Seth wouldn't have any hope. Nate had to keep to protocol.

"So back to my question," Vince said. "Who are you?"

"You don't need to know that. As soon as we get Seth help, I'll take you somewhere to catch a cab home."

"Oh, no. Not after this. I'm not letting anything happen to Kate."

"You don't have a choice."

Vince didn't say anything more as they drove. Kate hit the speed dial on Nate's cell but had to wait a long time for Harper's sleepy "Hello."

"Hey, it's Kate. We need your help."

"Shit. Fine. I'll be ready."

Kate blinked as she realized Harper had hung up without even asking what was wrong. She supposed the doctor would be ready for anything. Even a wound as serious as Seth's.

She remembered the blood on Vince's jacket, and she turned around to find him wincing as he shifted in the backseat. "You were hit."

"It's nothing."

"Your sleeve is covered with blood."

"I'll live. I'm more concerned about who the hell was trying to kill you. I'm pretty sure it was the Crips in the Buick, but I didn't get any kind of a look at the people in the Mercedes."

She turned away again, still concerned with his wound, but more anxious that he stop asking questions. She wanted to tell him it wasn't a gang, but then he'd want to know who it was, and she couldn't tell him that. She couldn't tell him anything.

"And while you're filling me in," Vince said, "you can tell me why ledgers from Kosovo were more important to you than your own life."

Nate's head jerked around, and he glared at her as if he could strangle her on the spot.

"Shut up, Vince. Just for once, be smart and shut up."

He did as she asked, but she knew it wouldn't last. She doubted he could have made any sense of the ledgers, but just seeing them put him in danger. Shit, Omicron must have known she was staying at his house. How else would they have found her?

Whether Nate liked it or not, Vince was involved. He was in danger, and there was no way they could simply let him go back to his life, even though he was a cop. A suspended cop. Why hadn't he told her?

But she couldn't talk it over with Nate, not in front of Vince. And not while Seth's life was slipping away. They couldn't lose him. She couldn't even think about that.

Nate slowed in front of an old two-story house. It had a small, fenced-in front yard and a driveway that led past the house to a freestanding garage. He pulled all the way to the back, then doused the lights. Turning to Kate, he said, "Get out your weapon until we get him in the house."

She nodded and took her Glock out of her pocket. She wasn't sure how much ammo she had left, but it would have to be enough.

They got out of the car, and Nate and Vince struggled to get Seth out of the backseat. He was a big guy, and it wasn't easy, especially because they had to be so careful of his hand.

Kate went up the back steps and knocked on the door. No one answered, so she banged harder.

Finally, the door opened. Harper, who Kate hadn't seen in almost seven months, was in her bathrobe. She looked like she was pissed off, but that wasn't unusual for Harper. Good thing Kate knew that, despite all the bluff, Harper was not only an amazing physician but would work herself to the bone if it meant saving someone's life.

"Seth's been shot," Nate said. They were almost up the stairs. "Is everything in place?"

"Yes, dammit. This way." She led them through the dimly lit house. Kate heard a TV upstairs. Harper opened the door under the stairs, then turned on the lights to illuminate the steps down. She went ahead, and Kate waited to take over the rear.

Once they had him on level ground, she looked at Seth. He was deathly pale, and she could hardly see him breathe. Her chest tightened and she said a prayer. He was such a good guy, and he'd been shot trying to protect her.

The basement had been set up as a trauma room. Nate had fixed it so that Harper could stay in this house, and he'd found a way to get all the supplies, everything necessary for an occasion such as this. They'd never used it before, but Kate could see Harper kept it immaculate.

"What happened?" Harper asked, going over to the washbasin to scrub her hands.

"They shot up his hand," Nate said. "He's lost a lot of blood."

Harper turned to Kate. "His file is on the desk. Look in there, and tell me his blood type and if he has any allergies."

Vince moved to a small nook by the back wall. He said nothing, but he watched everything, trying to make some sense of what he was seeing.

This basement was better equipped than half the emergency rooms in the county. There was a refrigerator with a blood supply, lighting good enough to operate by, every kind of medical gadget he could think of. There was even a second bed in the back, and next to that a wheelchair.

Were these people survivalists? Terrorists? What the hell had Kate gotten herself into? He'd been feeling guilty as shit since he'd looked in that box, but now he'd wished he'd confronted her right then and there. This was serious business, and something told him that the gangs coming after her was child's play in comparison.

The woman, Harper, was striking. Tall, he'd guess close to six feet, she had a strong face with intense blue eyes, short blond hair and a no-nonsense attitude. She was attractive, compelling. She looked like someone he wouldn't want to piss off. But then, so did the man glowering by the bed.

Kate helped Harper into a surgical gown and gloves. Then, the doctor went to examine her patient.

Vince took the opportunity to get close to Kate. He needed to understand this. And he needed to get her out. "What is this place?" he asked, keeping his voice low. "Who are these people?"

"I can't talk to you right now. I need to help Harper." She walked over to the bed. More to escape him than to help, he figured. He'd wait. He had nothing more important to do.

"HE SHOULD GO to a hospital," Harper said. She'd washed Seth's hand and taken a good look at the wound. It was bad. Really bad. The thumb was gone and so was the muscle structure beneath. She doubted even the finest surgeon could have done much. He wouldn't have much use of it, if she could save the hand at all. The deeper she looked, the more worried she became. "He needs a specialist."

"He's got you," Nate said. "And damn lucky for it."

She looked at him and shook her head. "It's not good. I'll do what I can, but he's not going to be using this hand for a long time, if ever."

Nate cursed and banged his head against the wall. They needed Seth. With both hands. With Kate going to Colorado, Boone and Christie following the trail of suspicious supplies leaving Montana, he would be on his own. With the new information about the storage facility, that was a huge problem.

He was pretty damn sure they were storing some of the chemical weapons there, but he had to make sure. If that didn't get him killed, his next step would. Somehow, they had to go public. Tam was still working on the antidote, but with their limited resources it was slow going. If Omicron sold any gas, a whole hell of a lot of people were going to die.

He looked back at Seth, and it killed him that his friend was in such bad shape. He had no idea how Omicron had found where Kate was staying. They'd had enough time to plan the assault, which didn't make sense either.

The cop, was he the leak? How in hell could they let him go, without knowing the truth? And what had he done to Kate to make her leave tonight, instead of following the plan?

"Harper, are you good?"

"Go. Just don't be too long."

Nate took Kate's arm and led her up the stairs. He knew the cop wasn't going to be quiet for long, and there were decisions to be made.

They went to Harper's kitchen, and he zeroed in on the bottle of whiskey she kept in the cupboard. He offered it to Kate, who declined, then he poured himself a shot. It burned going down. "What happened out there, kiddo?"

Kate took off her coat and sat down at the kitchen table. Her face was smudged with ash and almost as pale as Seth's. "Vince looked at the papers. He was trying to help. I've been something of a basketcase. He had no idea what he was looking at."

"Then how come Omicron knew you were there?"

"I haven't a clue. But I'd bet everything that he's not involved."

"I find that pretty hard to believe."

"I know. I think we should talk to him. If he is involved, then he doesn't understand what he's into. If he isn't, his life's in danger. Either way, we can't just let him go."

"Agreed. I'm gonna talk to him. Not you."

"Fine."

He sat down across from her. "Is there anything I need to know?"

"I think he's a decent guy, Nate. He just wanted to solve the murder of his friend. I don't believe he has any connection to Omicron."

"And snooping into your things?"

"Misguided, but well intentioned."

"I'll keep that in mind."

She touched his hand. "What's going to happen with Seth out of the picture?"

"I don't know. Let's solve one problem at a time."

She nodded. "It was just like that night, you know? In Kosovo."

He knew exactly what she was talking about—the night they'd escaped. His team was supposed to have gone to the lab, a bunker really, and retrieved all the data from every computer. After that, they were to destroy without prejudice. Which meant everyone in that lab was to have died. Only, the women, Harper, Kate and Tam, had proved to him beyond a shadow of a doubt that the mission was a lie. They'd been sent, by men he'd trusted, to kill American citizens. Innocent citizens. They were to have destroyed all the evidence that these men in their suits and their uniforms had conspired to build a chemical weapon, despite the ban, despite the consequences. Instead, Nate and his men, all ten of them, had mutinied. To his shame and deep regret, they hadn't been able to save the scientists. All of them had died that night, except for Tamara. And he hadn't been able to save all his men. When he dreamt, it was often of that night. When everything he'd believed in had come crashing down around him in a hell storm of bombs and helicopters. He squeezed Kate's hand. "Hey, at least tonight there were no bombs."

She smiled. "Yeah, I suppose that's a plus. But they sure brought a lot of firepower."

"Yeah, and we kicked their asses."

When she looked up, her eyes were wet with unshed tears. "I'll never get used to it. I killed two men. Me. An accountant. I shot them dead."

"Before they could do it to you."

"I know. There's a lot to be said for self-defense, but still. That we have to keep killing…"

"Not forever. I promise."

"I'm keeping you to that."

He leaned over and kissed her forehead. Then he rubbed the ash off her cheek with his thumb. "Count on it," he said. "We'll get through this. Now, we need to be there for Seth. And I've got to talk to your friend."

"Be nice."

"I'm always nice."

She laughed, and he was glad of that. There certainly wasn't much to laugh about.

VINCE LISTENED FOR footsteps as he watched the doc. She seemed to know what she was doing. He'd been to enough autopsies that the sights and smells didn't bother him, but he couldn't help wincing when he got a good look at the mangled hand. He wondered if the guy was left-handed. He hoped not.

"I need you to adjust the light."

He approached the bed. "How?"

"A little to the left. So I can see in the wound."

He did his best to give her what she wanted. "I'm Vince," he said. "Vince Yarrow. I'm a detective out of South Central."

"Nice to meet you. Now go away."

He went back to the dark corner and waited. Soon enough Kate came down but only to tell him to go on up to the kitchen.

He didn't want to leave her. He didn't particularly want to have this conversation with the man upstairs, either. "What's his name?"

"Nate."

"Who is he?"

She brushed his bloody sleeve with the tips of her fingers. "Harper, when you're done with Seth, would you take a look at his arm?"

"Have him take a number."

"Go on, Vince. And just be truthful with him. He's a good man."

He looked at her for a long time, wondering about her definition of a good man. He wondered how she'd described him to her pal Nate.

Upstairs, Nate had a bottle of whiskey on the table, and two pony glasses. Vince sat down, as tired as he'd ever been. "Name's Vince Yarrow, but I suppose you know that already."

"I do. And what I want to know, Vince, is who you've been talking to."

"Pardon me?"

"I need to know how those men found Kate. How they knew she was getting into a Yellow Cab at your place."

"I've been thinking about that. The men who killed

my friend knew Kate had seen them. They probably figured she could identify them. I don't know if they did some research on their own, or if they bribed someone to give them my address. My guess, they were staking out the house and followed the cab."

Nate poured two shots. "Well, that's a problem, Vince. Because the men in the Buick and the men in the Mercedes weren't part of a gang."

"What the hell are you talking about? I saw their do-rags. They were Crips, at least in the Buick."

"No, they might have looked like gang members, but they most definitely were not the real thing."

"Who were they?"

"I've got a real problem here." Nate leaned closer, and Vince could see a ferocity in his eyes. "The more I tell you, the worse it's going to be for all of us. For you."

"I can take care of myself."

"There's more at stake here than your life."

"I'll tell you right now, if you're doing something to damage this country—"

"We're not. I give you my word. We're not involved with any foreign nationals, and we're not out to make a statement. But we have information some very important people don't want us to have."

"Kosovo."

Nate nodded.

Vince tried to wrap his head around this information, but it wasn't easy. "What's Kate's role in all this?"

"She's the one who found the initial evidence. She got us involved."

"Kate?"

"She's a very bright woman, Vince, and she tells

me you're not in this up to your neck. I want to believe her."

Vince picked up the shot and drank it. It wasn't enough. "I have no idea how those people knew she was at my house."

"You haven't told anyone?"

"My boss. My partner. They would have no connection to anything you're talking about."

"Are you sure?"

"Yes, goddammit, I'm sure. I've known them both for years. We're up to our asses in gang warfare. It's enough, trust me."

"These people have money. Resources."

"There was an article in the *Times*..."

"I know."

"That's all I have to offer."

Nate looked at him for a long, unsettling time. "If you go back to your house," he said, finally, "they'll come after you."

"I'm a cop."

"Doesn't matter."

"Who are these people?"

"I don't think you should know more than you absolutely have to. Not only because I can't vouch for you, but because it's dangerous. But if you want to help Kate, you'll play this out carefully. Stay here tonight. Let us think this through."

"All right. For tonight, but not for you. For Kate. I want to hear this from her."

"Do yourself a favor. Don't press her. All of our lives depend on it."

"We'd better get down there."

Nate stood up. He held out his hand. "Nate."

Vince shook. "You're ex-military, aren't you?"

"How'd you know?"

"The way you were out there."

"Okay, so you're observant. That could be a plus."

"I'm also concerned about what all this crap is doing to Kate. She's pretty messed up over it."

"I'd worry if she wasn't."

Vince let the man's hand go. "I still have a friend who died at the hands of some brutal punks. I'm not about to let that go."

"One thing at a time, Vince. One foot in front of the other. Okay?"

Vince hesitated, but did he have a choice? "Fine."

Nate led him back down the stairs. Kate watched them each step of the way.

"He's going to stay tonight," Nate said. "And someone ought to look at that shoulder."

Kate nodded as she came to him, lifting her hands to help him off with his coat. "I'm still angry," she whispered. "You have no idea what you've gotten yourself involved in."

He turned to face her. "The only thing I'm involved in is you."

13

VINCE WAS RIGHT, his wound wasn't serious. Messy, but the bullet had grazed him, that's all. Kate used some wet gauze and cleaned him up, then covered the raw area with antiseptic. He didn't want a bandage, but she didn't listen. The troubling part was how he kept looking at her. As if he didn't know her.

It was, she supposed, because he'd seen her kill. He'd thought she was a nice person. Screwed up, but nice. What did he think of her now? Maybe that she was crazy, or a radical, or God knew what else.

She'd been so angry at him for sticking his nose in her business. Mostly because she knew exactly how dangerous that business was. Vince had enough trouble in his life without this. Without her. But it was too late now. He'd walked into her world, and she didn't see any way for him to walk out again.

"Hey," he said, touching her arm. "It's okay."

"No it's not. Nothing's okay."

"I'm sorry about your friend."

They'd gone up to the second floor, to the guest room down the hall from Harper's bedroom. Kate had tried to convince Nate that he needed to get some rest, but he wouldn't leave Seth's side.

As of a half hour ago, Harper had almost finished sewing Seth up. After that, she'd make sure he was comfortable, and she'd go to sleep in the second bed, in case he woke up.

Kate was awake only through sheer will. She'd had such a massive dose of adrenaline out there in Sunland that once it was gone she was shaking with fatigue.

"And," he said, taking her hand, "I'm sorry I upset you. I should have talked to you instead of barging in."

"I wouldn't have told you anything. I was going to leave tomorrow, uh, today, anyway. I hoped you wouldn't have to be involved. These people, they really want us dead."

"So it seems. What I don't understand is how you got involved. Were you in the service?"

"No." She sat down next to him on the queen bed. The room looked more like it belonged in a motel than in a home. Of course, there was no money for anything as extravagant as decor. Kate still wasn't sure how Nate had managed to equip the basement. She knew he'd made some money with a patent, but the stuff down there had cost almost a million dollars. Nate wouldn't talk about it, and Kate had learned to stop asking. "I worked for the United Nations. I'm… I was a forensic accountant."

"What the hell's that?"

"You've probably met some in your line of work. We investigate paper trails, follow the money. Then we put the information together in a way that allows attorneys and juries to understand our findings. It's not usually very exciting or dangerous."

"But not in Kosovo."

She shook her head, wondering how in the world she was going to find the energy to take off her clothes. Maybe she'd just sleep like this. "I found discrepancies. Big ones. Money being siphoned into accounts where they didn't belong. I was told to leave it alone, but that wasn't what I was hired to do. At the end of the line, I found Omicron. We didn't know they had a name back then, just that they were some operation loosely connected to the CIA."

"What were they doing?"

She debated telling him. But he was in so deep already, it probably didn't matter. "They'd developed a new chemical weapon. Incredibly nasty. We saw some of the victims. That's how Harper got involved. Anyway, they were planning on selling this stuff. From what Nate said, it was like the Iran-Contra deal. Except instead of guns and bombs, they were selling liquid death."

"Jesus." Vince shook his head, looking blown away. She knew the feeling. "Nate said you got him involved."

"Yeah. I knew he was in the Delta Force and that he had some kind of big secret mission. Him, Seth, Boone and Cade, and some others who didn't make it. They were told they were getting rid of the scientists and labs where the weapon was manufactured. Only we found out that the scientists they were supposed to kill were actually good guys. They'd been lied to by the same people. But they knew too much."

"So Nate and his men disobeyed orders."

"And from that moment on, we've been hunted. Our families think we're dead, and that's how it has to be. Omicron would use them to find us. They'd use anything."

"Wow."

"That's putting it mildly."

"How long have you been on the run?"

"Two years. And counting."

"Jesus. No wonder you hide in those lousy jobs."

She touched his face, so incredibly sorry, for everything. "If I testify, Omicron will kill me. But they won't stop there. We're actually making some headway. Those papers you saw, those will help. I'm trying to recreate the paper trail. Nate and Seth, they're working at finding out who's funding the operation. It's someone big, we just don't know how high this thing goes."

"Jesus."

"Nate's right. We have to take this one step at a time. If we rush, we blunder, and we can't afford that."

"Especially now that Seth is down for the count."

She nodded. "So the next step for us is to get some sleep. Stop thinking, at least for tonight."

"It's a deal. Are you going to stay here? With me?"

"I'd like to."

He smiled. "That's the best news I've heard all night." He leaned over and kissed her. It was gentle and sweet, and it wasn't a prelude to a damn thing. "Need some help with those jeans?"

"I'll manage. There are things in the bathroom. Toothbrushes, soap. Why don't you go first."

He nodded. "I'll hurry."

NATE JERKED AWAKE at the touch, his hand automatically going to his gun. He saw Harper and relaxed. "How is he?"

"He'll live, at least for tonight. I've cleaned the wound and stopped the bleeding." Harper stripped off her coat, and it was a shock to see her still in her bathrobe. "I hope I was able to save the rest of his hand, but there's no guarantee. There's nothing more to be done for now. Go get some sleep. You can use my room."

He got up. "Wake me if anything changes."

"He's going to be here for a while. Maybe tomorrow you could go over the house, make sure all the spy gadgets are working properly."

"I will. Thank you."

"Yeah. Now get out. I have to sleep."

Nate climbed the basement stairs, his legs heavy as lead.

VINCE CURLED HIMSELF around Kate, spooning her long, warm body. It had been a dizzying night, and he hoped he was more coherent after a few hours of sleep. He pulled her closer and closed his eyes.

Just as he was nodding off, she spoke. "There were two men," she whispered.

He had to strain to hear her, to stay perfectly still.

"They were Asians. One of them had a tattoo on his right cheek. It looked like a Chinese character. The other one had his sleeves pulled up and his arms were covered with tattoos. I could make out only one, three circles in a triangle. They had automatic weapons, and they were fast. It was overkill, but they didn't look angry. There was no expression on their faces. None. That's all I remember."

He kissed her neck. "It's enough," he said. "Thank you."

AT NOON, KATE WOKE UP in an empty bed. She sat bolt upright, her heart hammering in her chest. Then she heard the water in the bathroom and let out an unsteady breath.

It hadn't been a dream. Vince was really here, and Seth was really hurt, and she had reached a whole new level of fear.

Despite her anger yesterday, she knew she'd found someone in Vince who wouldn't be easy to shake. The last thing on earth she needed was someone else to care about, someone else to worry about.

He opened the bathroom door and when he saw her sitting up, he smiled as if she'd brought the sun. She looked at him, standing there so gorgeous wearing only a towel low around his waist. Good Lord, he was a fine, fine man.

"I hope I didn't wake you."

She got up, a little chilled being naked and all, but it didn't matter because a moment later she was in his arms and he was kissing all the heat back into her body. When she finally came up for a breath, she pulled him right back to bed.

Vince threw the towel on the floor and covered her with his still-damp, warm body. He kissed her deeply, his mouth minty fresh and wonderful.

He moaned as he ran his hand down her sides, gripped her by the hips and turned them both on their sides. She wrapped her leg over his, then kept right on going until she was the one on top.

He smiled up at her. "What's going on in that wicked mind of yours?" His voice was all raspy and sexy, and she got a chill just from listening.

"I thought we could, you know…"

"No idea."

She leaned over farther, until her lips were really close to his. "I guess I'll have to show you." Then she attacked, thrusting her tongue inside him as she pinned his shoulders with her hands.

He lifted his hips, letting her feel his hard cock, and she rubbed against him, anticipating his luscious reaction. She wasn't disappointed. He moaned low in his throat, gripped her with both hands and lifted her up until she got to her knees.

He bucked again, and she got the point. Reaching between them she positioned him by feel alone, then she hesitated. It was difficult not to just give in, his whimpers were so incredible. She rubbed him against her lips so he could feel how ready she was.

"Come on, woman. You're killing me."

"I'm having fun," she whispered, kissing his nose, his chin.

"This is not fun," he said. "It's torture."

"Big strong man like you. I think you can take it."

He lifted his head and captured her lower lip between his teeth. She got the point. She didn't want him to suffer. Much.

She positioned him perfectly then lowered her hips, thrilling at the feel of him filling her. He let her lip go and cried out, but her kiss shut him right up.

Closing her eyes, she moved slowly, deliberately, and his hands moved over her back and her sides, making her shudder.

The only problem was that in order for him to rub her on the right spot, she'd have to sit up which would mean she couldn't kiss him. She wasn't willing to do that. So once more, she reached between them, but this time, she only needed one finger. Her clit was hard and ready, and she rubbed it quickly as she continued moving up and down on his cock.

He kissed her urgently, and everything speeded up. A couple of moments later, and her body started to tighten, her muscles contract. She was going to come soon, and from the sound of him, so was Vince.

He beat her, but not by much. When it hit, he still had that look on his face, the one that made him fierce and vulnerable all at the same time. She let the shivers come as she spread her body over his like a blanket.

By the time her breathing had become even and slow, he needed another shower. But he didn't seem to mind. Not after she promised to wash his back.

NATE TOOK TWO MUGS of coffee down the basement stairs. As he figured, Harper was up, and she was standing next to Seth. He moved quietly, but she heard him and looked up. "Oh, thank God. Did you put sugar in it?"

"Two spoons."

"Good man."

He handed her a mug. "How's he doing?"

"Stirring. I've put more pain medication in his IV, so he shouldn't be too bad."

"Did you get any sleep?"

"A few hours. He woke up once, but he wasn't coherent at all."

"There's a lot to think about today. But I want to make sure I'm here when he wakes up."

"Stick around. It shouldn't be long." Harper went to the lone chair in the room and sat down. She was still wearing the same nightclothes, but her hair was uncombed and her eyes were tired and sad.

"What's going on with you?"

"Nothing until last night. Just working at the clinic, keeping my head down."

"I'm sorry we had to come here, but…"

"No. It's what I'm here for."

Nate drank some more coffee, his gaze on Seth. "How long is he going to be in recovery?"

"A long time, Nate. Even if he doesn't lose the rest of his hand he's going to have to wait until the wounds heal, then do physical therapy to find out what works and what doesn't. From the nerve damage, I'm guessing not much will. He'll probably need a prosthesis, and learning to use one isn't a simple matter of slapping it on."

Nate couldn't imagine Seth having to struggle with his body. Since the day they'd met, Seth had been in perfect physical condition. He considered his body his most important weapon. This wouldn't be easy.

"He'll stay here. I have a friend, someone I can trust, who works with prosthetics. And I'll find out what I need to know about his therapy."

"Can you do that? Along with your other work?"

"I have no life, Nate. None. I can do it."

He nodded, then heard the basement door open. Vince and Kate came downstairs. Kate's hair was still damp, but both of them looked like they'd gotten some decent sleep and a shower.

"How's he doing?" Kate asked.

"He'll be coming around soon. We need to decide some things."

Vince crossed his arms over his chest. "I'm not staying," he said. "I've got business to attend to. But if there's any way I can help you all, I'm happy to."

"Happy to," Nate repeated. "You're in their radar. It won't just go away."

"Fine. What do you recommend?"

"I'm going to give you a few things. You ever do a sweep for bugs?"

"Not personally, I've seen it done though."

"The machine I'm gonna give you is small, but incredibly powerful. If they've put any devices in your home, you'll be able to pinpoint the location and the frequency."

"You honestly think they've—"

"Count on it. I'm also going to give you a cell phone that can't be traced. Don't use anything else to contact Kate."

Vince looked down, maybe a little uncomfortable that Nate understood that something was going on between them. It didn't matter.

"If you notice anything weird, call. If you think you're being followed, call. Check for bugs every day. Kate'll show you how to mark your doors and windows to check for intruders."

"I have some pretty decent connections in the FBI. I can maybe do some legwork—"

"Thanks, but you have your own work. The more distance you can put between us, the safer you'll be."

"All right. I need to call my partner."

"Come on. I'll give you your stuff, and you can use that phone." He headed upstairs. "I'll drive you wherever you want, and you forget you ever saw this house."

When they were alone upstairs, he gave Vince the bug detector and showed him what to look for. Then he handed him the phone. But that wasn't why he'd wanted him up there. "You care about her."

"Yes, I do."

"She's leaving."

"What?"

"She's leaving the state. Tonight. We'd planned it for a long time. There's someone there who can take care of her. She's too visible. That picture in the paper put her, put all of us, in danger."

"She would have said something."

Nate walked over to Vince and put his hand on his shoulder. "She's a soldier, Vince. She knows what we're up against. She doesn't want you involved. If you care about her, you'll let her go. You'll say goodbye without tipping your hand."

Vince looked shaken, and Nate didn't blame him. It was a lot to ask of anyone, but this was a lousy time, with lousy options. "She'll be safe there?"

"Safer than if she stays here."

The detective opened the cell phone and dialed a number. "Jeff, I need you to come pick me up at the Denny's in Boyle Heights. I'll explain when you get there. Half an hour, okay?"

"I need to get back downstairs," Nate said. "I'll send Kate up." He started toward the back of the house, then stopped and pulled a piece of paper from his shirt pocket. "Here. It's my phone. Memorize it, then get rid of it."

Vince took it and stared at the number as Nate went down to the basement.

Kate was standing at the foot of the stairs.

Nate made a motion with his chin. "Go on. He's leaving soon."

She looked back at Seth, then she went up.

Nate heard a moan and he went to Seth's side, but Harper pushed him away. She listened to Seth's heart, looked in his eyes.

Another moan, and this time, Seth stiffened and tried to sit up. Harper's hand on his chest kept him in place. "What the... Oh, shit."

"Hey, man," Nate said. "Take it easy."

"What happened? Is Kate okay?"

"She's fine."

"My hand."

"You were shot," Harper said, in her best doctor voice. "It's bad."

Seth lifted his arm, the huge bandage not giving away much. "How bad?"

"Your thumb is gone. There's a lot of muscle damage."

"How long?"

She looked at Nate, then back at her patient. "A long time, Seth."

Nate could barely watch as Seth processed the news. He was a hell of a soldier, but Nate could see the pain written all over his face. "Don't worry," he said. "We'll get through it. You'll get through it."

"I need you to leave," Seth said, his voice as tight as a bow string.

"Sure thing, buddy. I'll see you in a bit." Nate turned and left, understanding Seth's request and goddamn grateful for it. He took the stairs two at a time, and when he got to the first floor he headed straight for

Harper's room. Once he was there, he sat down on the bed, and he bit his lower lip until it bled.

KATE LOOKED INTO Vince's face and told herself she wouldn't cry. She wouldn't. She'd known it would be over, that it should be over. They each had things to do, but not with each other.

"Jeff's meeting me."

"Sure," she said, trying to smile. "Sure. Are you going to be able to find those guys?"

"I think so."

"Even without my testimony?"

He nodded. "I should never have brought you into this."

"You were doing your job, Vince. I know how much Tim meant to you."

He studied her face, memorizing it, she imagined, as she was doing with him. It hadn't been long enough to feel this bad. As if she was losing half her heart.

"I want you to be safe," he said. "It goes against everything in me to walk away while you're in trouble."

"Oh, God, that's so nice. But it's just not possible."

He nodded. "This'll be over, right? You'll find out who's behind this, and then it'll be okay. You'll have your life back."

"Yeah. It will be over. And those bastards will pay."

"I don't know if I'll be with the P.D., but I'll be in L.A., okay? I'll be here."

She took his face in her hands. "Find those guys. Put them away. And then get the hell out of the gang detail, okay? Didn't anyone tell you it's dangerous?"

"Yeah, yeah," he said, and then he was kissing her, and it was just the hardest thing ever. The battle over her tears was lost, but she no longer cared. He was gone, she was going to Colorado, and there was no telling what would happen after that.

She pulled away and hugged him close. She brought her lips close to his ear. "My name," she whispered, "is Katherine Ashman."

"I won't forget," he said. "I swear. I'll remember for as long as it takes."

_14_

VINCE GOT INTO JEFF'S Ford and buckled in. His partner looked troubled as he pulled out of the Denny's parking lot, which wasn't a surprise. "What's going on?"

"What's going on is that you're hanging on to your job by the skin of your teeth. Emerson is getting every kind of flack, and he's about ready to just say screw it and fire your ass."

"I meant what's going on with the investigation."

Jeff grunted. "Baker seems to be the only one making any headway, and what he's got isn't going to make you happy."

"Shit, what now?"

"Look, don't shoot me. I'm only the messenger. Baker says he's got hard evidence that Tim was getting payoffs from five different meth labs."

"Evidence?" Vince felt his blood pressure climbing. "That's complete bullshit. Tim didn't have a nickel. If he was skimming from drug dealers, he'd have put it all into Purchase House, and he's been running that on fumes. What is this evidence he's supposed to have?"

"I don't know. He's not talking. At least not to us. I'm sure it'll be in the paper soon enough."

"I ought to go teach him a thing or two—"

"You ought to go home and shut the hell up. Where's your witness? Don't tell me you lost her."

"She's not going to testify. But I did get some information. It seems the Wu Chang were responsible."

"Wu Chang? They didn't have anything to do with Tim Purchase."

"I know. It doesn't make sense, but we have to look into it."

"We? You're suspended. You're not looking into squat."

"Don't you start giving me grief. Just because I'm not on the clock doesn't mean I can't ask questions."

"Fine, you don't want to work again, be my guest. But I'm still on the clock, asshole, and I know how to ask questions."

Vince stared out the window, wishing like hell he was still at that big old house with Kate. She'd be gone tonight, and then what? The best thing would be for him to lose himself in the work. Find the killers and put 'em away. He couldn't do that, at least not with the LAPD's blessing, so he'd have to do it without. Jeff didn't need to know. "Okay. Check around. See what you can find out."

Jeff shot him a look. "And you're going to butt out?"

"As much as I can, yeah."

"I've just gotten used to your sorry ass. Don't make me train a new partner."

That brought a smile. Jeff had to put up with a lot of crap from him. He never said a word, unless he thought something was too dangerous, and even then he'd usually go for it. Good partners were hard to find, and the two of them worked about as well as a man could hope for. "Sure thing. I'll keep my nose clean."

"Do that. I mean it. Emerson has completely lost his sense of humor."

"Haven't we all?"

"SHOULDN'T YOU BE getting ready?"

Kate didn't look up. She and Nate were at the kitchen table, in theory eating lunch, but neither of them seemed to have much of an appetite. "I've been thinking."

"About?"

"Not going."

Nate sighed. "I kind of figured this might come up."

"I have no business leaving," she said. Now, she looked·at him, wanting him to see how serious she was. "It's not right, and it's not safe to leave you here alone. I know you like to think you're a superhero, but, Nate, you're not. Just like Seth isn't."

He winced, and she held herself back from saying how damn tired he looked. "You're too visible," he said quietly. "We could have all been killed last night."

"I know, and I'm sorry about that, but they don't know where I am now, and that's just how it was before my picture was in the paper."

"It's not smart for you to stay. We have the place in Colorado for just this kind of circumstance. You go there, you're off the map. No one will find you. They won't even know where to start."

"They'll just keep looking for me here. Just like they keep looking for you. Nate, I can't. It wasn't his fault and it wasn't mine, but Vince is in danger now. I know he's not going to stop looking for those men that killed his friend. The safest thing for him would be to find them, as quickly as possible. Then he could disappear, too."

"You know they're going to be watching him like a hawk. Waiting for you to show up."

"Then I'll have to be incredibly careful, won't I?"

Nate shoved his plate aside and leaned back in the chair. "You care about this guy."

"I do."

"You willing to die for him?"

"It won't come to that. I suppose the answer would be yes, because I couldn't live with myself if I didn't help him."

"Help him how?"

"I have no idea."

"I have a lot on my agenda, Kate. That storage facility, for one thing. Seth and I were supposed to go check it out, make sure it's what we think it is. Now I have to figure out how to do that alone. And Seth, he's going to need a lot of help."

"I'll go with you to the facility," she said. "And I'll help with Seth. I'm not turning my back on our goals. I just don't want to see Vince get killed for something he had no part of."

"I don't suppose I could stop you."

"Nope. I'd appreciate your help. You know us forensic accountants aren't known for our superspy skills."

He laughed. "I'd say you've earned your secret decoder ring."

"Gee, thanks."

He looked at his watch. "I need to spell Harper."

"Why don't you go get some sleep. You look like hell. I'll take over downstairs."

"You sure?"

She grinned. "Don't even think of waking up until

you've had at least three hours of solid sleep. You hear me?"

"Yes, ma'am."

She got up and collected the dishes, putting them in the dishwasher before she headed down to the basement.

Harper was standing next to Seth's bed, but Kate didn't see what she was doing until she got close. As Harper was changing the bandage, Kate got a glimpse of Seth's mangled hand, which made her stomach turn. She kept her mouth shut and her face relaxed as she went to the other side of the bed.

"How you doing, big guy?"

His face was still far too pale, and at the moment, Seth appeared to be in considerable pain. "Shitty," he said.

"Sounds about right. Harper, can I do anything?"

"Not at the moment. I'm just going to finish this up, then I'm going to get something to eat. I'm even going to feed our friend here. You like chicken soup?"

"No."

"Too bad. That's what's on the menu."

He turned his head to the side, his lips pressed together tightly.

Harper wrapped the new gauze around his hand. "I'm giving you some pretty strong medications, and I don't fancy cleaning up after you vomit all over the place. So today, it's soup. It's got to be better than Meals Ready to Eat, right?"

"I'm not hungry," he said.

"That's why soup is the perfect answer," she said.

Kate admired Harper for her composure. Seth wasn't an easy man to deal with when he was angry, and God knew he had every right to be. But Harper didn't coddle him. She just did what had to be done. It reminded Kate of Kosovo. So many people there were wounded, with so few doctors, let alone proper medical equipment. But Harper had never let it get to her, at least not in front of the patients. Kate had seen her blow up a few times, and it had been something to behold. The woman didn't simply suffer no fools, she hit below the belt and didn't care who went down. Generals had quaked in front of Harper's wrath.

She couldn't wish Seth a better doctor. Maybe Harper wasn't a vascular surgeon, but she was incredibly well-trained for just about anything, and the woman never gave up. She'd get Seth fighting again.

When his hand was bandaged, Harper took his temperature with one of those ear deals, then peeled off her gloves. "How's the pain?"

"Bad," he said.

"Okay. I'll give you something, but then I'm going to get the soup, and you're going to drink it."

Once Harper was gone, Kate touched Seth's good arm. "I'm sorry."

He looked at her, and she could see the pain in his eyes. "What the hell happened out there last night? How'd they find you?"

"We think they figured out that Vince was babysitting and were planning to snatch me from his mother's house."

"They were dressed like gang members."

"I know. They probably wanted my death to look like a gang killing. Easy for them. No repercussions." She swallowed, and said it again. "Seth, I'm so sorry."

"Not your fault. You didn't shoot me."

She wanted to say more, to let him know how deeply she appreciated all he'd done for her, but there was a lump in her throat. The last thing she wanted to do was start bawling over his sick bed.

"So this guy, this cop. What's that about?"

"He's a stubborn ass, just like a couple of other men I could mention, but he's a good one."

"I see. What about your trip to see Cade?"

"Called off on account of I'm needed here."

"Be careful, Kate. They're not gonna be happy after last—" He coughed, choking on his words. His face got red. Just as she was about to run up and get Harper, he stopped.

"You need some water?"

He shook his head. His eyes were closed and he looked as if he might pass out any second.

She pretty much had given up on prayer. But for Seth, she pulled out all the stops.

IT TOOK AN HOUR and fifteen minutes to sweep his small apartment for bugs. He found three. It made him paranoid as hell, so he did the sweep all over again, this time the little light didn't flash. Still, he wasn't going to do or say anything in his apartment that could get him, or Kate, in trouble.

Once he was done, he fixed up some coffee and got out the day's *L.A. Times.* By the time he was finished reading Baker's article, he was so pissed he threw his coffee mug at the wall.

Not his brightest moment, but, dammit, every word of the article was a lie. All he wanted to do was find Baker and strangle him with his own intestines.

He just couldn't afford to be stupid. Not now. He might need his job back. He definitely couldn't do much good from jail. Still, he couldn't just sit on his hands.

He thought about going to Purchase House and seeing how things were there. Or to Chinatown to do a little soft investigation of the Wu Chang.

It wasn't a large gang, and its members normally didn't go in for wholesale murder. Why had they wanted Tim dead? Vince tried to remember if any of the newer kids at Purchase House were from their territory, but he hit a blank.

And why hadn't they taken credit for the kill? Something was off with this whole business. Vince didn't believe this was a territorial dispute. All his instincts told him there was another story, a deeper, more dangerous tale.

Shit, he couldn't go to Purchase House, could he? He had no car. Thank God he had no life, because if he had he probably wouldn't have such a nice amount in his savings account.

He grabbed his jacket, checked to make sure he had both cell phones, and, before he walked out of the apartment, he put a small piece of paper in the crack of the door, way down low. Jeez, this was going to be a pain in the ass. But if it helped Kate…

He thought about her the whole time he was checking out the used cars at Jimmy's Auto Sales. He made sure they knew he was a cop, so the price on the 2004 Taurus wasn't too bad. They did all the paperwork, and by the time he drove off the lot, he knew just where he was going. Not to Purchase House, not yet. He thought he might run over to see

Eddie, his informant. Maybe Eddie wasn't high this time. Maybe.

It wasn't all that simple to find him. He wasn't at the coffee shop. Or at his crib. Vince finally found him eating a slice of pizza from a sidewalk joint.

Vince parked half a block down, and he waited until Eddie had finished his slice, then he sidled up. "How you doin', buddy?"

Eddie didn't seem all that thrilled to see him, but he also didn't seem out of it. In fact, his eyes weren't dilated at all. "Shit, Yarrow. Why you want to do this on such a busy street?"

"Come on. I'll take you for a ride in my new car. Just make sure you don't have any grease left on your fingers."

Eddie, who was all of five foot eight and weighed maybe a hundred pounds, glanced about as if he was about to ditch, then followed Vince to the Taurus. He got in and looked over the new wheels. "Nice."

"It'll do."

"Can we go already? I don't want to be seen wit' you."

"Sure thing." Vince drove him about six blocks away and parked in an alley that wasn't used much, except by rats and stray dogs. He pushed his jacket back so the butt of his gun was visible, just making sure Eddie realized he wasn't interested in bullshit. "What have you heard about Tim Purchase?"

"Like I told ya. Nothin'."

"I let it go last time, Eddie, but that's not gonna fly now. So just get it over with. Tell me what you know."

"How come you think I know everything? People don't tell me all the shit that goes down around here."

"Eddie," he said, his voice a warning.

"Shit."

"What about this rumor that Tim was skimming off five meth labs?"

"That Mary? He wasn't doin' nothin' like that."

"No? Then how come a reporter says he's got evidence?"

"I don't know, man." Eddie was playing with the buttons on his jacket. Every time he moved, his sleeve would pull up, showing a deep line of tracks all the way to the wrist. "I never heard of no reporter."

"So, what have you heard?"

The junkie looked away, and his hand made an abortive gesture toward the door handle.

"You'd better tell me, Eddie. You know I can make your life a living hell."

"Too late, dude."

"You can't even imagine the hell I can come up with."

Eddie looked at him, then down at his hands. "You're not gonna believe me if I tell you."

"Try me."

"Just don't hit me, okay? It's just shit I heard. I ain't seen any of it wit' my own eyes, so it could be all bullshit, okay?"

"Okay, fine. Just tell me."

"I heard that it was a cop. From South Central."

Vince didn't speak. He didn't want to scare the snitch too soon. And if the quiet went on too long, Eddie would talk.

"I heard this cop was doing the skimming, only it was a lot more than five labs. He coverin' all downtown L.A. Chinatown, Koreatown, Little Vietnam. Even over

into some of them Crips and Bloods. Not the MS gang.
Nobody stupid enough to shake them dudes down."

"What cop, Eddie?"

"I don't know."

"Yes, you do. I can see you're lying. Do not screw
with me. Understand?"

"Why you don't believe I don't know? I'm just one
dude. I don't know everything that goes on out here."

"Eddie, I swear to God, if you don't tell me the cop's
name, I'm going to shoot you in your left kneecap.
Right here in my nice, new car. You understand me?"

"Don't, man," he said, his voice about an octave
higher. "Why you gotta get to the gun, huh? I ain't lyin'."

Vince put his hand on his holster and undid the snap.
"I'm losing patience, Eddie. If I don't hear a name, I
might just have to pop both your kneecaps. Hard to get
a date without any kneecaps."

"You promise not to hurt me if I say?"

"I promise. But you'd better be telling me the truth."

"It's what I heard, not what I seen."

"Okay, tell me exactly what you heard."

He touched the door with his hand, ready to run, and
Vince kept his hand steady on the butt of his weapon.
"It's your partner, man."

"What?"

"Don't shoot, don't shoot. I told ya. It's what I heard.
I ain't seen him."

"Who told you it was Jeff?"

"I don't know. I heard it from three different dudes.
One of them rumors, you know? When I buyin'."

"Names, Eddie."

"I don't know names. I don't write that shit down. It's just, you know, talk."

"Get out."

"Hey, you ain't gonna leave me in this alley."

"Get out, now."

Eddie cursed, but he got out of the car, his jacket swinging behind him, his ratty knit cap low on his forehead. He slammed the door shut just as Vince cranked the engine. Eddie jumped out of the way as Vince jammed it out of there.

It couldn't possibly be true. Why would the street be saying it was Jeff? No way his partner was skimming. Couldn't happen. Jeff was a good cop and a better partner.

So what the hell was going on? Who was doing all this talking, and why?

He needed to get to the bottom of this, and that led him straight to the Wu Chang.

15

THE MESSAGE CAME THROUGH on the phone Vince had gotten from Nate. It was in text, and it was an address, followed by a number. He hadn't been sure what the number meant until he pulled up in front of the Skylight Apartments.

He parked the Taurus on the far side of the parking lot, not at all sure he wanted to do this. It couldn't be good news. Nate had made it pretty damn clear that communication between them would be limited to life or death situations. Which could only mean...

He got out of the car and locked it, then headed toward apartment 104. He knew this area of L.A., though not this particular building. It was nondescript, boxy, rundown. The paint had chipped on the door, and the numbers were crooked.

He hesitated before knocking, thinking once again that he shouldn't have left Kate. He should have told Nate to go screw himself and taken her with him. He had friends, connections, he could have protected her against the CIA, the gangs, everyone. Losing Tim had been a tremendous blow, but to lose Kate. *Jesus.*

He checked to make sure there was no one watching him, then realized it was useless. Anyone could hide themselves on this moonless night. They could be in one of the other apartments or across the street. Sitting in one of those parked cars. So he knocked on the door, bracing himself for the worst.

He got the best, instead. Kate opened the door. Kate, with her long hair pulled back, wearing a dark green shirt and smiling so hard it made him ache.

"Get in here," she said, pulling at his arm.

The second he was inside, she shut and locked the door, and then she was in his arms and he was kissing her. He ran his hands all over her back, her sides. She was supposed to be in Colorado. Or dead.

He pulled back to look at her face, to make sure she was really all right. "I didn't think I'd see you again."

"Plans changed. I'm staying."

"Nate said it was too dangerous for you here."

"It's always dangerous, and I can't leave him to fend for himself."

"So, you're going to step in for Seth?"

She nodded. "As best I can."

He ran his hand down her back and drew her closer. "I don't know. Maybe I could help."

She touched his cheek with her fingertips. "I'm sure you could, but you've got it backward. We want to help you."

"With what?"

"Finding out who killed Tim."

He pulled away from her. "What are you talking about?"

"Come on. Sit with me." She took his hand and led him past the couch in the studio apartment, to the bed that was in the back. Vince wondered who lived there, who'd left a pair of cowboy boots on top of the dresser, next to a copy of *Newsweek*.

The bed was good and firm, the same size as the one at Harper's, and had been made the same way he made a bed. Kate sat on the end, and he joined her, still not sure what this was all about.

She smoothed back a loose strand of hair, and he learned all over again how achingly beautiful she was. "It would have been bad enough if you were just facing the gangs, but now you've got Omicron on you, and there's no way you should have to deal with them alone. I want to help. We want to help. Let's nail those gang bastards, okay? Let's get them off the street, and then…" She looked away, to the door, then down to her hands.

"And then?"

"Omicron's not going to give up. They'll keep watching you for as long as they have to. You won't know where they are or if they'll try and do more than just watch. God, I'm sorry. I wish like hell I'd never been in that room. I dragged you into this, and I can't stand back and do nothing about it."

"Jesus, Kate, do you think I'm going to let you put yourself in danger for me? Are you nuts?"

"I'm not going to put myself in any more danger than I'm already in. I'm serious about this, Vince. Let us help. We're damn good at this spy stuff, trust me."

"I do trust you. But I have no idea how you can help. I know the gangs, I know the territory." He stood up and walked over to the window. Though the drapes were closed, he peered between them to make sure no one was lurking nearby. "I talked to one of my street snitches today. He was remarkably coherent, considering. He…"

"What?"

He turned around to face her, and it struck him that he didn't want to say the words out loud. "He said it wasn't Tim who was skimming from the meth labs. That it was Jeff."

"Your partner?"

He nodded. "I don't believe it. Not for a second. What I don't understand is why that's the word on the street. Junkies are notoriously bad at lying. Well, to each other, at least. They don't remember shit from one minute to the next, so they end up blurting out the truth. So who's out there saying this? First they're feeding the *Times* lies about Purchase, now Jeff. I don't get it. It doesn't make any sense."

"Is there anyone else out there you can trust?"

"Trust? Gangbangers? Junkies? Not likely." He came back to the bed and sat down with a sigh. "Goddammit, Kate. I don't want to believe Jeff is involved. Not in this."

She took his hand. "But…?"

"I don't know. When Eddie said his name, I got this feeling in the pit of my stomach. Jeff's a good partner, and I've never seen him do anything to rouse suspicion."

"Well, you must have a reason for feeling the way you do. You were right about me, remember? You knew I'd seen the shooting. Anyone else would have bought my story."

"I don't like it. I don't like the whole thing."

"It's awful, I know. You can't turn away from this. Not if you ever want to trust Jeff again. We'll get to the truth. You and me. Together."

"If something happens to you…"

"It won't. I told you. We're really good at this spy stuff."

He nodded. "I imagine you are. You shouldn't have to be. I hate it. I hate that you're involved in any of this. I keep thinking there's someplace you can go that they won't look for you. Where you can have a life."

"I don't want just a life. I want *my* life. I deserve to have my family, my old friends. They stole it from me, and I can't ignore that."

He cupped her soft cheek. "I worry."

"Tell you what. Let's not either of us worry right now. We have this place until midnight, and I've learned to appreciate gifts where I find them. So let's not waste any more time, okay?"

Vince couldn't argue with that. He leaned over and kissed her as his thumb stroked her perfect skin. All he wanted to do was keep her safe, and he wasn't at all sure he could.

Her hand went to the back of his neck, her fingers spread in his hair. He shivered at the touch. Still, he wanted so much more.

He pulled back, let her go. "I thought I'd never see you again."

Kate shrugged. "You never can tell."

"The problem is, I didn't bring anything with me."

She grinned. "No problem. Stay right there." She got up and disappeared into what he assumed was the bathroom. He kicked off his shoes, put his jacket on a chair. Kate came back just as he was pulling off his shirt.

"Ta-da." She held up a large, economy-sized box of condoms.

"Who lives here?"

"Friend of Nate's."

"Friends are good."

She nodded, then joined his efforts to get naked. "Very good."

He was done before her, so he figured he should help. Stepping behind her, he undid her bra, but he didn't take it off. He slipped his hand under the cups instead. He loved her breasts. They were small but perfect, with these great, responsive nipples that were as erect as his cock. He brushed the tips with the palms of his hands, taking great pleasure in her sigh.

They swayed from side to side as he nibbled on her neck. She tasted warm and delicate, like a rare fruit. She leaned her head to the side so he could have better access and he caught her earlobe between his teeth.

She hissed and rubbed her backside against his growing erection.

"Take off your panties," he whispered.

"I'd love to, but you have to let go."

"I don't think I can."

She chuckled, and he felt it in his hands, his chest. "You need to think about the big picture. The grand scheme."

"That's true," he said. "Although there's a lot to be said for the details."

She turned around in his arms. "I want you inside me," she said softly, just before she kissed his chin. "I want to watch your face when you come."

He let go, and then he fell to his knees and slipped her panties down her long legs.

She stepped to the side. While he was down there, he kissed that wonderful spot just below her belly button. God, she was so incredibly soft. His hands went around her, and he stroked her beautiful cheeks, then down the back of her thighs. He licked her flesh, moving his mouth to the edge of her curls.

She had her hands in his hair, and she scratched his scalp, which was an amazing feeling. More amazing was when her legs parted, the most enticing of invitations.

Kate closed her eyes as Vince kissed the top of her mound, then inch by inch lower. She shivered, anticipation making her moan. Then his hard tongue slipped inside her and she inhaled sharply with the sensation. Slow, tight circles and she gripped his hair so he wouldn't move.

He captured her clit between his teeth, then sucked, hard, and it was so intense she rose on tiptoe. The pleasure came through her in waves, and when he flicked his tongue fast, then faster, she shook with the rising swell of tension. "Don't stop," she said, getting more desperate with each second. "Oh, God."

He kept her on her toes, flicking, sucking, over and over until she exploded with an orgasm that made every muscle in her body spasm. And still he didn't stop. Not until she pulled him away.

He looked up at her, his smile as wicked as his talented tongue. "Something wrong?"

Still gasping as the shockwaves continued to rock her, she shook her head. "No. I just want more."

"Okay," he said, putting his mouth back on her pussy.

She laughed. "No. I want you. Up here."

"Hmm," he said, kissing her before he stood. "Okay. I'm here. Now what?"

She reached down to take hold of his cock. "Gee, I don't know. Any ideas?"

He groaned and pushed himself into her hand. "Bed. Now."

She agreed. She let him go, and he pulled the bedding down so hard it came all the way off the mattress.

They laid down, and when he kissed her, she tasted herself on his tongue. It felt naughty and sexy, and she just couldn't seem to get enough of him, touching his back, his sides, then his hard, thick cock.

He moaned again, then pulled away from her kiss. "Condom."

She reached over him to the box on the night stand and pulled one packet out. With amazing speed, Vince took it from her, ripped it open, then rolled it on. She would have laughed if he hadn't taken her by the shoulders and flipped her onto her back.

Looking up into his eyes, into the way he was looking at her, she realized that they had to win this battle. This war. Because she needed to be with this man. And not just until midnight.

SHE SAT IN THE CAR and focused on the laptop. It was just after 2:00 a.m., and Nate should be coming out of the warehouse in the next five minutes. They'd gone over the plan a dozen times, and while she would have preferred being more active, she knew that watching the guards was critical.

After Nate had found the location of the facility, he'd cased the warehouse and placed a small camera in front of one of the side windows of the storage facility. He'd monitored the thing for the last week, watching every pass of the security vehicle. He'd given himself fifteen minutes to get in, check the containers and get out.

He'd missed one pass by security, but the escape window was damn tight.

All Kate could do was wait and tell him if anything went wrong. As the seconds ticked, she got more and more nervous, wishing like hell he would come out already.

How did these guys do this stuff without having heart failure? She was terrified Nate would get caught, or that the warehouse had booby traps, or that she'd get caught, and he'd have no way home.

And then thoughts of Vince would invade, and she'd have to shake him off so she wouldn't lose focus, but it was hard, because when the thoughts came she was flooded with such warmth, with such a feeling of safety that made absolutely no sense in her universe.

Still, she was the lookout, and she couldn't risk a moment's inattention. Their lives depended on the timing, on everything moving like clockwork. She'd give Nate another two minutes, and then, as he'd made her promise, she'd leave.

With one minute to go, and her heart beating like a bird's, she saw him. It wasn't easy, him being all in black, including his face. But she knew where to look, and damn, there he was, climbing down a line so slim she couldn't even see it.

She'd never turned off the engine, and now she put the car in gear and rolled quietly to his position. She put the computer in the backseat, leaned over and opened the door. A few seconds later, he was inside, and they were out of there.

They didn't speak until they were two blocks from the facility. "How'd it go?" she asked.

"It's the gas. They've labeled all the boxes as indus-trial solvent. The canisters were the same design as the ones we saw in Kosovo."

"How many?"

"The warehouse is half-full. They've got enough juice in there to wipe out the population of Chad." He opened the glove box and took out a rag and a jar of face cream. He started cleaning the black off, his movements agitated, his breathing harsh. "Tell you what. This stuff scares the shit out of me. One canister breaks loose, and there goes everyone in a thirty-block radius, if it's not a windy day."

"What's next?"

"I don't know. Obviously, we can't let them sell it."

"Can we talk about something else now, or should I wait?"

He didn't answer for a moment. "Yeah, sure. Why not?"

Kate told him about her conversation with Vince and her plan to help him. By the time they reached Harper's house, Nate was in.

VINCE WALKED INTO THE STATION knowing that he was persona non grata and not giving a rat's ass. Jeff was sitting at his desk, as expected, and Vince gave nothing away as he went to his own desk.

"You sure you want to be here?" Jeff asked. "Emerson's not going to be happy."

"He'll survive. I'll go talk to him in a while. First, I need to know what you've found out about the Wu Chang."

"Nothing. A big fat zero. I spoke to Charley Yang yesterday, and he said there was nothing happening between the gang and Tim. And he hadn't heard anything about Tim skimming any meth labs. All of this is out of left field. Baker is either making it up, or he's got a source who is."

Vince opened his top drawer and looked at the accumulated crap. An old picture of his ex-wife. About twenty pens, most of which didn't work. There was nothing organized about his personal space, yet when it came to case files, he was Mr. Meticulous.

Now Jeff, on the other hand, didn't have a paper clip out of place. He never came to work in a black suit with blue socks. Never had a hangover, never spilled any coffee in his keyboard. Jeff needed order, which was a damn strange thing for a detective. There was no order in the world of gangs. Damn impolite, they were. Killing each other with spectacular messiness, marking up every damn wall in the city with their graffiti. Jeff would have been a good accountant, or maybe an actuary. Yeah, that would have fit him just fine.

One good thing about his orderly life was that Vince knew that if he was doing something "hinky" with money, he'd have it written down. Not here, but at home, on his personal computer. That's why Vince had given Kate his address and told her about the iffy lock on the back window.

She and Nate should be in the house by now. They'd have to get into his computer, which was sure to have a password protection. Knowing Jeff really goddamn well, he suspected Jeff would probably use the same password he used here. If not, Kate had said not to worry about it. That Nate could get in through a back door.

Still, he was nervous and he felt guilty even thinking that Jeff would have anything to do with meth dealers.

Because if Jeff had skimmed the money, then he'd been the one giving Baker the false information about Tim. Worse, he'd be directly connected to Tim's death.

All Vince wanted was to know. To get this horrible feeling in his gut to go away.

Talking to Charley Yang was a logical move, but Charley was on the periphery of the Asian gang scene. In order to get what he wanted, Vince would have to get out there himself, go to Chinatown and talk to the Cho brothers. They were dangerous, mostly because they weren't that bright. However, they were connected in the Chinese community. Their thing was racketeering, setting up betting rings and taking their share off the top, which was why it didn't make sense that they'd been the shooters.

He couldn't move on to the Cho brothers yet, though. Not until he knew.

"I'm gonna go talk to the Captain," Vince said. "You'll be here when I get back?"

"Are you kidding? I wouldn't miss the fireworks for anything. I do believe Emerson is going to kick your ass."

"I'm pretty sure you're right. Do me a favor and call an ambulance if you hear me scream."

Jeff laughed, then went back to his paperwork. Goddamn, there was always paperwork. At least Nate and Kate didn't have to mess with that.

SHE BOOTED UP THE DESKTOP computer as Nate went through the desk drawers. He was extremely careful, putting everything back exactly as he'd found it. He'd taken digital pictures of the desktop and each drawer when he'd first opened them so that he could make sure there were no mistakes.

Both of them were wearing thin latex gloves. No fingerprints would be left behind. Nothing to clue Jeff in that he was under suspicion.

After the boot stopped, Kate clicked on the financial program icon. It was, as Vince had predicted, password protected, so she typed in Jeeter45, but it didn't work. "No go."

"Okay, let me get in there. You finish up with the drawers."

They switched places and Nate got busy with his keyboard magic. She was amazed at how organized the drawers were. Organized and completely innocent. If Jeff was doing something illegal, he hadn't left any evidence in his desk. She had her doubts about finding anything recorded in his books, but Vince had been adamant that Jeff would keep some kind of record.

She finished her search. "Nothing."

"Go look in his bedroom. Check for false bottoms in his drawers. And don't forget the camera."

She headed toward the back of the house, taking careful steps and feeling guilty. Breaking and entering—that was a new one. Whatever else she could say about her life after Kosovo, she was certainly expanding her resume.

VINCE WAITED FOR the Captain's face to change from bright red to light red. He'd been hollering for ten minutes straight. Vince would have acted more chastened if he wasn't worried that Jeff was going to leave.

He'd told Kate the truth. After he put away those responsible for Tim's death, he was through with gangs.

No more. He didn't want to meet any more drugged out informants, or find babies shot up by drive-bys, or memorize tattoos and gang symbols. He wanted out. He was qualified to go to Homicide, but no—that would be just as bad as gangs. Administration, now that had a nice ring. Although he wasn't sure he wouldn't go stir crazy riding a desk.

"Are you even listening?"

He thought about saying no but nodded instead. "I told you, Captain. Baker's printing lies. Whatever evidence he has is bogus."

"And I told you it's none of your goddamn business. What part of suspension don't you understand? It doesn't mean you get to hide a witness. In fact, hiding a witness can get you put in jail, which would be real interesting for you. I'm thinking you wouldn't last a night."

"She's not a witness. She didn't see anything."

"You said she was in the suite when the murder went down."

"She was behind the bar. She didn't see the killers."

Emerson leaned back in his chair, looking at Vince through narrowed eyes. "What the hell are you doing here, Vince?"

He didn't like lying to Emerson. The Captain was a good man, and he'd always been fair, and he'd stood up for Vince many times. Nevertheless, there was so much at stake on this one, there was no choice. "I left some crap in my desk. And I wanted to check up on the investigation. Just for my own peace of mind."

"Well, for my peace of mind, do it over the phone. I don't want anyone thinking you're here because you're working. Because you're not, right?"

"Not me. I've been drinking beer. Getting laid."

"Get the hell out of here."

Vince went to the door, but Emerson's, "Vince," stopped him.

"Yeah?"

"We'll find out who did this. I swear."

Vince nodded and headed back to the bullpen. Jeff was still there, still working on the paperwork, and it occurred to Vince that he was being a jackass. There's no way Jeff was involved in any of this. No possible way. The man was a friend and a good cop. There was something else going on, something Vince was missing.

"Hey, you still have an ass," Jeff said.

"I get that, you know," Vince said. "Captain chewing my ass out. Yeah. Funny."

"I thought so. Are you ready to buy me lunch yet?"

"Give me two minutes. I have to hit the john."

"No sweat."

Vince headed down the hall, his doubts growing with each step. Jeff had covered for him too many times to count. He'd walked into situations that should have gotten him killed, just on Vince's say-so.

He made sure there was no one in the bathroom and called Kate on his cell.

"Yes?"

"Kate. Tell me I'm wrong, okay? Tell me you haven't found anything, and I'm just being paranoid."

He waited for her response. But there was only silence. "Kate?"

"Vince…"

"What? What's wrong? Are you okay?"

"I'm sorry, but we found something."

His stomach clenched, and for a minute he thought he might throw up. After a few deep breaths, he said, "What did you find?"

"There's a bank account. In the Cayman Islands."

He leaned against the wall as he closed his phone. Jeff. His fucking partner. The one man he was supposed to count on. Closer than a brother. How? Jeff knew Tim Purchase. He'd been to dinner with the man, had barbecued in Tim's backyard.

It was everything he could do not to go right to the bullpen and shoot the bastard between the eyes.

No matter what, Jeff was going down.

16

SETH COULDN'T BELIEVE how sore he was. Not just his hand—that made sense—but the rest of him. Everything hurt, and he got tired walking the eight steps back from the bathroom.

He looked at his bandaged hand and cursed. Even with the thick gauze, he could see it wasn't his hand anymore. Where there should have been a thumb, there wasn't. No control, either. He could barely move his whole arm, and when he did there was pain as fierce as any he could remember. Everything felt too heavy and stiff.

Someone opened the upstairs door, and from the footsteps he knew it was Harper. She'd been up with him most of the night, and he figured she'd still be sleeping. When she came around to his bed, the exhaustion was clear on her face.

She looked at the cup by his right hand that she'd left two hours ago. "You didn't drink your soup."

"I wasn't hungry."

"I don't care. Consider it medicine, and just get it down. You need the protein."

He nodded, which made his headache worse.

"It's almost time for more meds. And sleep."

"Are you going to sleep, too?"

"Sure."

"You don't lie well."

"I know. It's a curse."

Something else was going on here. Her posture, the way she looked at him. It wasn't about soup. "Well, then I guess you'd better just tell me the truth." He already didn't like it. Fear, like a giant fist, squeezed his chest. "Go on."

"I can't save your hand. The nerve damage is too extensive."

He closed his eyes as the pronouncement hit him, first in the gut, then in the heart. "You want to cut off my hand."

"It'll save your life."

"And what life will that be?"

"Yours. It will take some adjusting, but you'll be able to function quite well."

"Quite well for who? A soldier needs both hands, Harper. Both hands."

"There's nothing that says you have to—"

"That's all I am. That's all I've ever been."

"And you'll still be exactly who you want to be. You're right-handed. You can still use a gun. You have your strength, your experience, your judgment. The prosthetics they make now are incredible. In time, you'll master the use of it, just like you've mastered so many other difficult things."

She didn't get it. Not at all. He'd felt as if he'd been a soldier his entire life, and it was his body, all of it, that made him who he was. Rage swallowed him whole, and he cursed his aching body because he could hardly get out of bed, let alone throw the chair through the wall. "No. You're not chopping my hand off. You hear me?"

"Just think about it, okay? The nerves are mostly gone, and there's already necrosis. It has to be done, Seth."

"Fuck you, Harper. I said no."

"All right," she said, as if she were talking to a child. "Calm down. We'll talk about it later."

"No, we won't. You'd better get out of here." Even his legs were shaking. No goddamn way he was letting her cut off any part of his body, but especially not his hand. He had work to do, and he couldn't do it as a cripple.

"I'll go in a minute," Harper said from the counter. She came back to his bed with a syringe. She got his IV and pushed the needle in, taking her time with the pain meds as his hand, his one hand, trembled on the white sheet.

He wouldn't be awake much longer. With any luck, he would just stay asleep forever.

BAKER'S HOUSE WAS IN Toluca Lake, off Barham, and when Vince pulled up in front, he saw a kid's bike leaning against the garage door and a folded mitt lying on the driveway. He didn't know Baker had a kid. Too bad for the kid.

He got out of the car without his weapon, his badge in the glove box. He ran a hand through his hair as he walked up to the front door. It was just past six-thirty, and he didn't want to be here, but there were steps to be taken, and he was the only one who could take them.

He rang the bell and a boy answered. Vince guessed he was about eleven. He seemed surprised, as if he were expecting someone else.

"Who are you?"

"I need to speak to your father."

"Yeah, but who are you?"

"I'm a cop."

"Where's your badge."

"Look, just tell your father that Vince Yarrow is here."

The boy shut the door. Vince wondered if he should ring the doorbell again, but before too long the door swung open. Baker, looking at him as if he was the last person on earth he wanted to see, stood barring Vince's entrance. "What the hell are you doing here?"

"I have some things to discuss with you."

"If you think I'm going to drop the case—"

"I don't give a damn about the lawsuit. This is a lot more important."

"What is it?"

"I don't particularly want to do this standing on your front porch."

"Tell me what it's about, and then I'll decide where we talk."

"I know who's responsible for Tim Purchase's death."

Baker continued to eye him skeptically, but, after a bit, he stepped back and let Vince inside.

The house was nice, and Vince figured he'd been way off on what reporters earned. There was a grand piano in the living room and a lot of art on the walls. There was no sign of a kid—or wife, for that matter, as he was ushered into a home office.

Books lined two full walls, and there were pictures of Baker all over what was left. With the mayor, with celebrities, with the governor of California.

Baker nodded toward a wooden chair as he sat in a swivel chair in front of his computer.

Vince opened his mouth, but the reporter held up a hand. He got a small tape recorder off the desk.

"Hold it," Vince said. "This is off the record. If you don't agree to keep my name completely out of anything that should arise out of this conversation, I leave."

"I can't agree to that until I know what you're going to say."

Vince stood and headed for the door.

"Wait. All right. Whatever we say for now is off the record. If you're trying to jerk me around…"

"That's the last thing I'd want to do, trust me."

"Sit down, already, and tell me what the hell you want."

Vince took his seat. "The allegations about Tim Purchase are fabricated."

"What makes you think so?"

"First, I knew the man. Well. There isn't a chance in hell he'd have anything to do with drug dealers. It was totally outside his character."

"Haven't you learned yet that we don't know shit about anyone? Even our closest friends?"

Vince winced. "I've learned something about that, yes, but it's not true about Tim."

"I can't just drop it because you think Purchase was a swell guy."

"No. You can investigate the real reason for his death."

"Which was?"

"I believe he discovered that a detective out of South Central was skimming off at least five meth labs. And that he threatened to go public. I also believe that this detective hired members of the Wu

Chang to go to the hotel and kill him. And that framing Tim is simply a device to keep all eyes off the true perpetrator."

Baker stared at him for a while, then shook his head. "Why haven't you busted this guy?"

"It's not time yet. I learned of the evidence in a somewhat dubious manner. I can't use it to arrest him. In fact, I can't even use it to get a warrant."

"So you want me to do the dirty work."

"You're good at it."

Baker smiled. "I probably should be insulted."

"Yeah, you probably should."

"All right." Baker put away the tape recorder but got out a notepad. "No one will see this. Ever. So tell me what you've got."

This was the really hard part. Telling this man, of all men, that his partner had gone south. It hurt, deeply, but the course was set. "It's my partner. Jeff Stoller."

Baker blinked a few times, but he didn't interrupt. Not even to ask how Vince knew about the bank account in the Cayman Islands. He wrote in shorthand, and he took down everything. By the time Vince had laid it all out for him, he felt as the world he'd known had vanished forever. Nothing would ever be the same again.

"What about that witness of yours?" Baker asked.

"She didn't see anything."

"I don't believe you."

Vince shrugged.

"I can't just drop what I have on Purchase. Not until I verify that everything you said is true. Even then, I'll have to have proof that the evidence was planted."

"What do you have?"

"An envelope ready to be mailed to Tim Purchase. With ten thousand dollars in it."

"That's nothing. That's bullshit. It wouldn't stand up in court."

"There's a confession by one of your Wu Chang boys to go along with it."

Vince bit back his curse. "Just follow up on what I'm telling you. You don't need the witness. The evidence you want is in Stoller's computer."

"Your partner, huh? That must be a blow."

Vince stood. "I've given you everything I can. The rest is up to you."

"I'll see where it leads. But don't for a minute think I'm going to just take your word for any of this."

"Just do your job."

Baker got up and took him back through the living room to the front door. Vince was halfway back to his car when Baker shouted.

He turned.

"This also doesn't mean I'm going to drop the assault charges."

"Get Stoller," Vince said. "That's all that matters."

KATE WIPED HER EYES as she went to Harper's back door. As a precaution she had her gun in her hand, but she knew it was Vince, so she opened the door as quickly as she could and slammed into his arms. His hard body felt so strong and good and safe.

"Hey, hey, what's the matter? Kate?"

She hugged him a little longer, then she pulled back. "It's Seth."

"Oh, shit."

"Harper can't save his hand. She has to amputate."

"Oh, man. I thought you were going to tell me he was dead."

"I think he'd prefer that. It's bad, Vince. He's refusing to let her operate, but he'll die if she doesn't."

"Let's get inside."

She hadn't even realized they were standing in the open door. Vince walked into the kitchen, bringing her with him. He went to the coffeepot and poured a mug, which he handed to her. Then he got one for himself.

When they sat down across from each other at the table, she felt a little better. "The thing is, he's a soldier. He was one of the toughest men in all of Delta Force. He doesn't know anything else."

"It's gotta be a hard blow. But I've seen him. He'll still be a soldier. He'll just have to accommodate the new circumstances."

"But will he?"

"I can't answer that. I guess he'll have to see what he's really made of."

"I just feel so horrible for him. If I hadn't left that night—"

"Hey. Stop that right there. You're not to blame. The men from Omicron shot him, not you. They wanted to do you all harm. It's not your fault."

Kate shook her head. It didn't matter what anyone said, she knew that Seth had been shot protecting her. That would never change.

"Are the three of them downstairs?"

"No. Just Nate. Harper's asleep. She's exhausted."

"I'll bet."

"What about you? I've been thinking about you all afternoon. I'm so sorry about your partner."

"Yeah, me too. I can't let him get away with it. I went to the press. To Baker. I told him everything."

She inhaled sharply, but he shook his head. "Not about you. Not about Omicron. He doesn't know how I got the information about Jeff. And everything I did tell him was off the record."

"That's good."

"Good, but not enough. I've still got to figure out what to do about the Wu Chang. They killed Tim, they gave Baker false evidence, and they have to pay."

"Won't Baker's investigation put them in prison?"

"I don't know. Without a witness, there's nothing to put them in that hotel."

A new stab of guilt shot through her. "I'm sorry—"

"I didn't say it to make you feel worse. I said it because it's the reality now, and I've got to do what needs to be done without getting you involved."

"You can't go after them, Vince. You're still suspended."

"I don't care."

"Well, I've been thinking about all of this," she said. "I have an idea, but I want Nate to hear it, too. Drink your coffee. I'll be right back."

She kissed him quickly, then went to the basement. Nate was leaning on the counter, his arms folded over his chest, watching Seth sleep. His eyes were red, his hair a godawful mess and he looked five years older.

"Hey," she said, keeping her voice low.

"Who was at the door?"

"Vince."

Nate nodded. He still hadn't looked at her.

"I want to bring him down. I have some ideas on what to do about his problem, and ours. But I need to talk to you both about the feasibility."

"Fine," he said. "Seth's not gonna wake up for a while."

She went over to where Nate was standing. "Can I get you something? A drink? Coffee?"

He finally looked at her. "I'm not hungry or thirsty. I'm just pissed. I want those Omicron bastards so badly I can taste it."

She smiled. "Maybe we can get them. Not all of them, but enough to make a dent."

"Bring it on, superspy."

"I'll be right back."

"Hey, Kate?" he said, just as she hit the stairs.

"Yeah?"

"Coffee would be good."

"I'm on it."

IT WAS JUST SHY OF midnight when Vince finally got Kate alone in the guest bedroom. His head was still reeling after hearing her plan. "You know," he said as he unbuttoned his shirt. "When I first met you, I thought you were gorgeous."

"Really? How bizarre."

"Don't even try and pretend you don't know."

She was taking off her clothes, and for a moment, as her shirt came over her head leaving her in her plain white bra, he forgot what he was saying. Those fools who thought fancy lingerie made a woman sexy. They'd clearly never seen Kate.

"Well, thank you for the compliment."

"That wasn't the compliment."

"No?"

"No. What I was trying to say was that while I do think you're gorgeous, I also thought you were smart. Sweetie, I had no idea."

Kate grinned. "It's okay. I'm a sure thing."

He laughed. "You're anything but. I can't predict you, I stand in awe of the way your mind works. You're a surprise every time I see you."

Now she was in her bra and panties, which were also white, and looked so pure and sweet on her body he could have dropped to his knees in thanks. Especially when he thought of how the innocence of her underwear hid the fire that burned underneath.

"No more," she said, running her nails down his bare chest. "Make me forget everything. There's no tomorrow. There's nothing else out there. No pain. No death. No lies."

He grabbed her hands by the wrists and held her still. She struggled, but not much. Her eyes, even more than her words, made him hard, and to show her what she'd done he pushed his cock against her belly.

Her lips parted as her eyes fluttered closed. He wrapped her hands behind her back and he kissed her brutally. Her moan told him it was just what she wanted.

His tongue, as hard as his cock, thrust into her willing mouth and she struggled there, too. The scrape of her teeth, and then a bite, just hard enough to make him crazy, forcing him to move her backward until she hit the edge of the bed. Lifting her hands, he made her tumble, him on top of her. Now his weight held her down. She squirmed underneath him as he nipped and licked the soft skin just under her ear.

"Let me go."

"No."

"Vince," she said, shaking the bed as she tried to bump him off. "Let me go."

"No. I'm not ready."

"I am."

"Too bad." He grinned, then took her lobe between his teeth.

She understood the meaning of the gesture and she quieted down, except for her breathing, which, despite his weight, moved his chest along with hers.

He wanted that bra off. And the panties. But in order to do that, he'd have to let her hands go. What she'd do with them was a little scary, but then, what was life without risk?

The moment he released her, she shoved him so hard he ended up on his back. Quicker than he'd have thought possible, she climbed on top of him, straddling his hips. "You are a very foolish man," she said.

Her hair tumbled forward, and she brushed it over his face. Now her hands grasped his wrists, and her smile became an evil delight. "I can do anything I want."

He lifted his hips, which wasn't easy. "Then why don't you take off those panties."

"Maybe."

"What can I do to convince you?"

She hummed as she mulled it over. "I think you can say—" She stopped, her mouth open, her eyebrows raised, as if her own words had shocked her.

"Say that I love you?" he asked quietly.

She sat up, releasing him, and a second later she was

off him, off the bed, standing in her old-fashioned underwear like a lost child.

He got up and pulled her right back into his arms. "I do," he said. "I didn't know it before, but I do. I love you. You're amazing and I can't even imagine how I didn't see it."

"Don't," she said, as she pushed him away, her pale hands firm on his chest. "You can't. We can't."

"Why not?"

She looked up at him with huge, wet eyes. "Because after... After tomorrow, I can't see you again."

"What are you talking about?"

"Don't you understand why we're doing this? To give you time to get away. You can't stay here, Vince. They'll kill you. These people will hunt you down and kill you."

"I've dealt with killers before."

"Not like them. They're professional assassins. They're going to kill thousands. You think one cop is going to stand in their way?"

"You're still here."

"And Seth is going to die unless he has his hand amputated. Is that what you want? To stick around and watch me get murdered? It's a miracle we're all not dead. I can't be there when it happens to you."

He stepped back, shocked at her intensity, at the way she was staring at him. "I'm not going to walk away from you."

She picked up her shirt and pulled it over her head. When she looked at him again, the fire in her eyes was gone. "Well, I'm going to walk away from you."

He couldn't believe she was serious. After all this, after all they'd been through, she was just going to leave? He couldn't imagine not speaking to her, not sleeping with her. "No," he said.

She had her pants halfway up her thighs. "What?"

"No. This isn't over. You're still in danger."

She sighed, then pulled her pants up the rest of the way. She didn't even look at him until she was fully dressed. When she did, he knew she wasn't going to listen to him. There was such sadness in her eyes, it couldn't mean anything else.

She sat next to him on the bed and studied his face. Her hand, cool and soft, went to his cheek. He fought the urge to take her by the shoulders, to shake some sense into her. "I wish it could be different," she said. Her voice broke and she cleared her throat as she turned away. "This isn't my choice. If I had my way…"

"We can make this work."

She shook her head. "It's over. When I'm free. When there's no one hunting us, we'll see."

"We'll see," he said. "That's it, huh? We'll see?"

She stood. "It's the best I can give you. I'm sorry." She leaned over and kissed him gently on the lips.

He reached for her as she walked away, but his hand dropped uselessly to his lap.

17

TWO MINUTES AFTER KATE was supposed to have arrived at his mother's house, Vince had convinced himself that something had gone wrong.

He was tired after a mostly sleepless night alone, while Kate had been down in the basement, switching shifts with Harper and Nate. He knew Seth was getting worse, but he also knew that if he hadn't told her he loved her, she would have spent the night with him.

He couldn't take it back now. Nor would he want to. It wasn't his way to lie, not about something this important. If they never saw each other again, at least she would know the truth. And if he died tonight, which was far more possible than he cared to admit, he'd feel proud of loving Kate. He didn't take the prospect lightly, or bandy the word about. Love and death, those were the things that changed a man. All the other stuff could shift him around a bit, but the big two? They went to the core.

He wanted to get up, to go to the window, but that wasn't part of the plan.

Nate had cleared the way for Kate to enter and exit. He'd made sure Omicron's bugs were intact in Vince's mom's house so that they'd take the bait but that no one was actually nearby. In fact, Nate was outside right now, with his surveillance equipment and an automatic rifle. But they'd all agreed that Omicron would be listening, not watching.

Of course, this was just the first part of what was going to be one hell of a long night. But if Vince thought about everything that had to fall into place, he would go crazy. All he had to worry about for the moment was Kate's arrival and their scripted conversation.

He heard a car outside, but he waited to stand until Kate knocked on the door. The second he saw her in the flesh, he wanted to call the whole thing off. The woman made him ache. Not just for her touch or her scent, but in fear for her safety. He knew, clearly and with no hesitation, that if he had to choose between taking down Jeff and the Wu Chang and saving Kate, there was no contest.

He pulled her into his arms and she clung to him. He inhaled deeply as he buried his face in her hair. When he kissed her, her cool lips turned warm and his heart raced for a whole new reason.

Too soon, it was time to start the play. She stepped back, giving him a quiet nod.

"What are you doing here?" he asked.

"I want to go see it," she said.

"What?"

"Purchase House. I'm going to be leaving tomorrow, and I don't want to go without paying my respects. I have something in the car. It's not much. Just a couple of baseball mitts, but I figured the kids might like them."

"I don't know, Kate. I appreciate the thought, but I don't know how safe it'll be there. Maybe you should just give the mitts to me. I'll make sure they get there."

"No. It's a huge part of your life, and I want to see it with my own eyes. So I can remember when I'm gone."

He pulled her back into his arms. "How'd you get to be so stubborn?"

"Me? Stubborn? Nah. Just determined."

He laughed. "Okay. Let me get my keys."

"I'll follow you," she said. "I don't want to leave the car here."

"Okay. But don't lose me. That's a really bad part of town."

"Right," she said, playing her part like a seasoned actress. He wondered if she was nervous. If she had her gun ready. Probably under her big coat. Hell, she was used to this kind of thing.

Once he was several blocks from the house, he got out his cell phone. Not the one Nate had given him. He dialed Jeff's number, hating his partner more than he ever would have thought possible.

"Stoller."

"Hey, it's me."

"What's up?"

"Can you meet me at Purchase House?"

"I guess. Why?"

"I've got a solid lead on Tim's killers. But I have to check something out before I make a move. If it's there, we can go after them tonight."

"We? You're still suspended."

"Okay, then, you. But I tell you, Jeff, I'm pretty damn sure I know what happened. I want you there to get the evidence."

"Who is it you think did it?"

"The Wu Chang."

"They didn't have anything to do with Tim."

"I know. I can't go into it now. Just get there. Half an hour, okay?"

"Okay. I'll be there."

Vince hung up the phone and put it in his pocket. Everything was in play as of right this minute. He hated that it was going to come down at Purchase House, but it was the only thing that made sense. Tim's desk was there, his papers, his books. If there was anything to find, he'd find it in Tim's office.

Kate was still close behind as he drove slowly on surface streets. He knew that Nate had taken off the minute they'd left, and that he'd be in place, across the street from Purchase House, by the time he and Kate got there. All three of them had bulletproof vests on under their clothes. Vince just hoped they wouldn't need them.

KATE ADJUSTED HER EARPIECE and murmured a quiet, "Nate?"

"I'm in position," he said, his voice so strong it was as if he was speaking from inside her head.

"Roger that." They were at Purchase House, which looked more like a warehouse than anything else, with a small sign above the double front doors that read: Purchase House—A Place To Grow. There were lights on in the parking lot and lights above the entrance, but the place seemed deserted. She knew that wouldn't last.

Vince was already out of his car, heading toward her. It was hard just looking at him. As always, he looked as if he'd just tumbled out of bed. His hair was all over the place, he hadn't shaved, and to her he was the best looking man she'd ever seen. Everything about him made her want more. His long legs, that high, round butt, his perfect chest. But none of his physical attributes came close to the attraction of his heart and his determination. She admired him so.

If only...

No. She wasn't going to go there. Hadn't she learned her lesson yet? That she was stuck in this purgatory until they destroyed, once and for all, Omicron and all it stood for. That for her, the regular rules didn't apply. She couldn't get a good job, she couldn't live in a nice place, she couldn't even have a real bank account. And, most certainly, she couldn't have a man like Vince.

He opened her door and she stepped out into the cold November night. Her gun was in a holster that placed the weapon squarely in the small of her back. Driving wasn't terribly comfortable, but that was nothing. She needed to be able to get to it in a heartbeat, which meant the ankle holster wasn't right. She grabbed the bag where Nate had put the baseball mitts and steeled herself for what was to come.

Vince took her hand and headed toward the entrance. He had a set of keys, and she wondered if he'd always had them or if he'd gotten them just for tonight. It didn't matter. The key turned and they went inside.

He turned on a bank of fluorescent lights and she got her first good look at the place. It was huge, with a vast open area in the middle. On the right, there were offices, all of them with big glass windows. On the left was a kitchen and rows of tables. There were easels, bookshelves, toys, a row of computers on the back wall. She saw rolled up mats, bright pictures on the walls, boys' and girls' bathrooms. It was easy to see how this place drew in children, especially from this neighborhood. Here it was warm and safe, with good food and respect served daily. A haven. And the man who'd created it was lying dead because a bad cop wanted more money.

"Heads up," Nate said. "Jeff's coming in. There's another car behind him, but it's heading toward the back."

Kate stiffened as she relayed the information to Vince. "There's an exit over there," he said, pointing toward the office. "That's how we get out. Remember what I told you about the escape route?"

She nodded. "Over the fence, then across the street to Nate's truck."

"You ready?"

"No, but let's do it anyway."

He gave her a kiss, and she could tell he wanted to say something else, but he stopped and led her to Tim Purchase's office. Again, he used the key ring, and once they were inside, he set the bag on the floor. He unlocked the door leading outside, but left it closed. Then he moved in front of the ugly metal desk, pulling her beside him.

"They're going to attack from there," he said, pointing toward the bathrooms. "I'm thinking Jeff will keep us occupied while they sneak in. Right under our line of sight."

"Omicron hasn't ever shown much finesse," she said. "They'll burst in the front door with all the firepower they can muster."

"Don't wait to see who gets who. Just run like hell and make it over that fence. It's not tall, but it'll slow them down if they put up a chase."

Kate nodded, her heart thumping in her chest. She

wanted to get out her gun, but it was too soon. Jeff still had to come in and distract them. God, she hoped she'd been right about all this. It had sounded good on paper, but what if the Wu Chang knew about this exit? What if Omicron decided not to waste time and just blew the place up?

"Stop it," Vince whispered.

"What?"

"You're thinking too much. Just relax. Be ready."

She smiled. As much as she wished it was all over, she dreaded that moment more. With the end of the Wu Chang, with Jeff in jail and Omicron subdued, at least for the moment, she'd have to say her final goodbye. It was simply unthinkable.

The front door swung open, and Kate got a look at Jeff Stoller for the first time. He was smaller than she'd expected. Wholly unremarkable. His hair was a muddy brown that matched his overcoat. His face seemed pasty with a bright splash of pink on either cheek. The only thing that made him stand out was his smile. As broad and pleasant as a kindergarten teacher's. No wonder no one suspected him.

"What have you got there, Vince?" Jeff called out. "I thought it was just going to be the two of us."

"Yeah, well, Kate wanted to see the place."

"Kate, huh?" Jeff walked inside the small office and stood square in the middle of the door. "So you're the famous eyewitness."

"That's right," she said.

In her ear, Nate spoke again. There were four men coming in from the back entrance. Gang members. And it looked like Omicron had arrived, only they were coming in dark. Again, four men, wearing black, crossing the parking lot from the east. She could hear a soft shuffle, and she knew he was adjusting his rifle. She had to fist her hand so she wouldn't go for her Glock.

"I can see why Vince has been so careful with you."

"Pardon me?" she said. "I don't understand."

"You're just his type." Jeff turned to smile at Vince. "So what's this evidence you found, buddy?"

Vince moved around the desk, reaching into the bookcase to pull out a large volume. She couldn't see the title, but she did see that from that position, he had a good bead on Jeff and everything against the back wall.

It would happen any second. The Wu Chang would come in and be faced with the killers from Omicron. She imagined it would be quite a battle, but she wouldn't stick around to make sure.

"I've been busy," Vince said. "Talked to a couple of people. Word is, it wasn't Tim skimming the money at all."

"You didn't hear?" Jeff said. "There was ten grand coming his way from one of the labs."

"Ah, but my sources tell me that the envelope was planted in order to get the scent off the real scumbag. That Tim found out who was making the deals, taking the money from the meth labs, and that he was going to come forward."

"Who'd you get that from? Eddie?"

"Among others."

Jeff shook his head. "Too bad. I heard Eddie was killed yesterday. Some dispute over a vial of crack."

Kate could feel Vince's anger, even though he was standing on the other side of the office. She just hoped he didn't explode before the time was right.

"You heard that, did you?" Vince asked.

"Seems to me that bad things keep happening to your sources," Jeff replied, looking straight at her. "They all either end up dead or disappear."

"Now!" Nate said, so loudly she jumped.

Jeff's eyebrows lowered as he lost the bright smile.

All at once, the doors in the back and the front of the building slammed open. She reached behind her and pulled out the Glock, but not before Vince had his weapon in his hand.

Gunfire went off in the cavernous space, so loud it hurt. Jeff lunged at her, grabbing her coat with one hand and shoving his own weapon into her belly.

As the men outside the office sprayed each other with death, as screams became louder, Kate tried to get her gun between herself and Jeff before he pulled the trigger. Only, Jeff was knocked flat by Vince's body, flying over the desk and knocking them both against the wall.

He swung his fist into Jeff's face, hard. Then again. Red blood spattered against the beige. Above them, the glass shattered and Kate ducked behind the desk.

It was bedlam, and it was all she could do to not scream. But Nate's voice was in her head, and he was screaming at her to get out. That he could see the door, and where the hell was she?

But she couldn't leave, not when she couldn't see where Jeff's gun was. She looked over the desk and saw bodies lying on the great concrete floor. An Asian boy, not more than seventeen, his mouth and his eyes wide open. An Omicron assassin, his hand resting on top of a red toy truck. But there were still men alive, still men shooting. She counted two men from Omicron, and three from the gang. One of them, of the three, was one of Tim's killers.

But her attention was pulled back to the struggle in front of her. Jeff had gotten the better of Vince, and he was hitting him, hard, with the butt of his gun.

She stood and aimed her weapon at Jeff, but if she shot him now, there was every chance she'd hit Vince, too. In order to get a clean shot, she'd have to move, get to the open side of the office.

Her plan shattered as she watched Vince's body drop like a stone, his head hitting the floor so hard it bounced. Then, before she could react, Jeff was on his feet. She took aim at his heart and pulled the trigger, but her aim was knocked off course by a tremendous crash as the rest of the office windows were blown apart. Jeff rocked back, screaming in pain. He looked at the blood coming from his arm, then at her. In a move that made her gasp, he dove onto the desk, straight at her before she could lift her gun again. His head rammed her stomach and she hit the bookcase behind her. She gasped, the wind knocked out of her. Jeff got off the desk and looked back at Vince, who still wasn't moving.

Kate couldn't breathe, but she knew she had to move, to get to her gun, before Jeff found his. She inched to her right, peering over the edge of the desk. There it was, near the far wall. Her chest loosened and she breathed in a deep breath, one that cleared her head as well as her lungs. Just as she was bending to get the Glock, a hand, Jeff's hand, grabbed the back of her neck and pulled her up. "Not a chance, lady," he said, his words slurring from a deep cut on his lip.

"Everyone knows," she said. "You can't escape.

They know about your bank account in the Caymans. They know you hired the Wu Chang to kill Tim."

"Good thing I have enough to retire," he said. He pulled her toward the exit with his good hand. He held his weapon in the other, blood from his upper arm dripping down to streak his fingers.

A bullet screamed past her ear, and he jerked her to the side. Another scream, this from a man, not a bullet, and someone else was dead.

Jeff thrust her outside, and she prayed that Nate was watching, that he could get a good shot from the building across the street. She tried to remember what she'd learned in hand-to-hand training, but he was shoving her in front of him, holding her arm in a viselike grip, the gun pressing into her back. Yes, he'd hit the vest, but at this range, there was little chance she'd survive.

He pushed her to the left, away from Nate, away from Vince, who was bleeding on the floor. Was he still alive? Would Omicron or the gang find him lying there and put a bullet in his head?

"Move," Jeff said, his voice little more than a snarl.

"Kate."

It was Nate. The earpiece was still there. Did he see her?

"There's another car. Omicron. They're coming around the back."

Well, this was it. If Jeff didn't kill her, Omicron would. Well, she couldn't stop Omicron, but this bastard? He was wounded, she wasn't.

He pushed once more, and Kate dropped and spun, using the weight of her body to bring Jeff forward and over. He cursed and she went for his gun. She found it, but he still had a grip, and he wasn't about to let go.

He hit her with his left hand flat against her cheek. Then again, jerking her head and filling her with pain. The third time, she must have relaxed her hand, because the gun was gone.

Shots rang out, over her head. She ducked, but Jeff hit her once more, slamming her head back, wrenching her neck, and when she opened her eyes again, she found the weapon, three inches from her face. He snarled, and she squeezed her eyes shut, waiting for it.

But that shot didn't come. Jeff's body flew off to the pavement, and above her, bloodied but whole, stood Vince.

Another shot came from above, and then it was quiet.

Kate backed away as Vince kicked Jeff's arm viciously, sending his weapon scuttling across the ground. "You stupid bastard," he screamed, blood spitting out with the words. "You killed him, you prick. You knew he was good, and you fucking killed him. He was ten times the man you'd ever be."

"Righteous asshole. You never understood a goddamn thing." Jeff was crawling backward, using his own good arm, but Vince moved with him, standing over him with bruised fists and unbelievable fury.

Kate hit the wall, and she used it to get to her feet. Behind them she saw bodies. Three bodies. All in black. Their weapons littered the pavement and their blood glistened in black pools. Thank God for Nate.

"I understand this," Vince said, his voice low and trembling. "You're going down. You hear those sirens?

They're coming for you. You're going to jail with all the gangbangers and all the murderers and rapists and thugs you arrested. There won't be a safe place. A night you don't find out what it is to be someone's bitch. You got that, you insufferable traitor? The best you can hope for is a shiv in the back. And you deserve every minute of hell."

Jeff had moved all the way back to the fence. His mouth dripped blood and his eyes were filled with panic. Just as Vince was leaning down to lift him by his coat, Jeff's gun whipped out from behind his body. He pointed it at Vince's face, the gun shaking.

Kate moved left, ready to launch herself into Vince's body. But then she saw Jeff wasn't the only one with a gun. Vince shot him in the heart. One clean shot.

Jeff crumpled. His gun fell with a clatter, his head hit the edge of the fence. Kate nearly passed out with relief, but the exit behind her flew open.

She had no idea who it was, just that there was another gun. Another shot.

Then a hand gripping her arm, pulling her hard, making her climb over the small fence. She was running, and it was Vince next to her, urging her on, his steps ragged as he struggled to keep up with her.

Somehow, they made it to the truck, and Nate was already behind the wheel. They crouched in the back seat breathing loudly as they dripped blood on the upholstery. The sirens got louder as Nate pulled out of the driveway, heading toward home.

Vince struggled up, pulling her up with him. He lifted his filthy shirt to the side of her mouth, dabbing at the blood.

Kate rested her head against his, as his arm moved around her shoulder.

They were alive. They had won. It was over.

For now.

_18_

VINCE ACHED IN PLACES he'd forgotten he had, and every move had him gasping just a bit. When he looked at Kate, at the bruises on her face, her swollen eye, he wished he could kill Jeff all over again. He'd trusted that man with his life.

"We should just go to Harper's," Kate said. "You look like hell."

"I'll live."

"We should get this done," Nate said. He was driving the speed limit, on surface streets, attracting no attention. "You two have to get moving tomorrow."

Kate sighed and shifted a bit in Vince's arms. "Thank you," she whispered, lifting her fingers to brush against his split lip. She winced. "I'm sorry you had to go through that."

"He was my problem."

"Omicron wasn't. And now…"

"Now, you need to rest and heal. Take care of Seth. Get back to your work."

She nodded. "Where will you go?"

"Let's talk about that after."

Closing her eyes, she rested her head against him once more. "After is good."

When she was comfortable, Vince thought about his next task. He was going to make a bargain with the devil. Baker was a self-aggrandizing ass who wanted his Pulitzer more than he wanted the truth. What Vince had to offer might just be his ticket. Which would serve them all well.

It was late, and Vince didn't really want to wake up Baker's wife and kid, but they'd survive. Kate wouldn't, unless he played his cards right.

"You remember the storage facility address?" Nate asked.

"Yeah."

"And the name I gave you?"

"I've got it all. You don't have to worry."

"I always have to worry."

Vince smiled, then regretted it immediately as the move pulled at his battered lip. "What's next for you?"

"I'm going to keep watching the Omicron offices. See if they've stashed any gas anywhere else. Try to figure out who's the top dog."

"In other words, the same old, same old."

"Yeah, I suppose so."

"It was a good thing you were up on that roof." Vince looked down at Kate. Her eyes were still closed and he hoped she was sleeping, not just resting. "I didn't think about a second team, which was stupid. They did that in Sunland."

"Yeah. They don't like to take chances." Nate turned onto the street where Baker lived, then parked a few doors down. He put the truck in Park, but he didn't turn off the engine. "When I see you coming down the walk, I'll come get you. Don't dawdle."

"I want this over more than you do. Trust me."

He hated to move Kate, but there was no choice. She blinked at him, but the next second she was wide awake. "We're here already?"

"That we are. You stay safe. I'll be back in a few minutes."

She lifted her chin for a kiss, which he gave her. A very soft kiss. If it didn't hurt so much, he'd have laughed. The moment he stepped out of the car he lost his sense of humor.

This little talk he was about to have was every bit as important as the Purchase House operation. He had to convince Baker to play ball.

The walk to the door seemed a whole lot longer, and not just because Nate had parked down the street. Every muscle hurt. What was worse was the new awareness that there was a skilled, silent enemy out to kill him. They had his name, his address, everything about him, and they considered him dispensable. His badge meant nothing. His history of exemplary service meant nothing. They simply wanted him dead.

The porch light was on, but he was sure no one was up at this hour. He rang the doorbell, waited half a minute, rang it again. Then again. Finally, he heard movement behind the door.

"Who the hell is it?"

"Vince Yarrow."

The door flew open. Baker, in a striped bathrobe, looking exactly like a man who'd been forced out of bed, glared at him. "What the hell?"

"Get your notepad."

"What?"

"I said, get your notepad. You're going to want to write this down."

"Are you kidding me? Do you know what time it is?"

"Yeah, I do."

Baker stood for a moment, and Vince could see the debate in his eyes. "This better be the best damn story I've ever heard," he said, stepping back to let Vince inside.

"It is."

KATE STARED AT the reporter's door from the backseat. She couldn't lean back or rest, not until Vince was by her side, safe and sound.

"Kate?"

"Yeah."

"You know this is it, right? That tomorrow, you're gone?"

"I know."

"Do you really?"

She shifted her gaze to Nate. "Believe me. I get it."

"Hey," he said. "You care about the guy. I know that. Leaving's gonna be a bitch. I wish I could make things easier for you, but—"

"I'm sorry. I didn't mean to get snarky. I just hate it, that's all. I hate it so much."

"You got to keep your eye on the prize. This will be over. If Baker does his part, it'll be over a lot sooner."

"If."

"Vince is a pretty persuasive guy. I'm thinking Baker's gonna play ball."

She agreed, but she still wanted to hear it from Vince. Long minutes ticked slowly by and nothing happened. No cars, no cats, no paper boys. It was as if everything outside

the car was frozen in time. The quiet became nearly un-
bearable. She turned away from the window. "Nate?"

"Yeah?"

"What's gonna happen with Seth?"

Nate sighed. "He's going to get better. He'll stay with
Harper. She's the only one who can help him at this point."

"I don't think Seth's going to like that much."

"He's a soldier. He'll do what he has to."

"I know she did the right thing, but God. What a
horrible choice to have to make."

"A damaged Seth is a hell of a lot better than a dead
Seth. He'll get over it."

"I hope so."

"Hey." Nate put the car in Drive and inched forward.

Kate saw Vince walking down the path. She couldn't
tell if it had gone well or poorly, not from his posture.
But that was probably because he was hurting.

When the truck stopped, she pushed the back door
open, and Vince got in next to her. Nate took off the
second the door shut.

"Well?"

"It's fine," Vince said.

She shook her head. "Details."

"Yeah. Well, I told him all about the storage facility.
Of course I didn't say anything specific about you guys,
but I gave him the rundown about the chemicals, and
what Omicron had planned. He didn't believe me, not
at first. But then I told him to look up some key players
online. You were right, Nate. There's evidence, but you
have to know where to look and how to read between
the lines. He agreed to investigate, and if it all pans out,
he'll run the story."

"What about the business with Jeff?"

"He's all over it. I told him he might want to get down to Purchase House, that there were some interesting things going on down there. He made a phone call to confirm."

"What about us?" Kate asked.

Vince turned so he was facing her. He smiled, not giving a damn about how it hurt his lip. "He's going to print that you aren't a witness any longer. He's not going to look for you, or write anything else about you, except that you know nothing."

She fell back against the seat. "Thank you."

"I told him one more thing."

Kate leaned toward him. "What?"

"I told him I quit. That I was off the case. Off any case. I told him he could confirm that with Emerson first thing in the morning."

"I thought you were just going to transfer. Get out of gangs."

"I am out of gangs. I'm out of the whole game. I've left a message for the Captain. I don't even have to go back to hand in my badge and my weapon. It's over. I'm done."

"What are you going to do?"

Vince kissed her once again on the lips. Then he looked over at Nate. "The thing is, I'm a pretty handy guy. I know how to use a weapon, and I know something about covert operations. So I figured while Seth was laid up, Nate might need a hand."

"No," Kate said. "You can't."

"Why not?"

"It's not your fight."

"They're trying to kill the woman I love. What part of that isn't my fight?"

She stared at him in the dim light of the car. He looked like he'd been run over by a truck, and he hadn't gotten that way from being a cop. "It's unrelenting," she said softly. "There's no part of your life that's normal. Not your name, not your home. You can't call anyone you know. It's so hard, and it never stops. I can't let you do that."

"They already know who I am. I'll be safer with you guys than on my own."

"That's not true."

"You don't know that."

"Uh, guys?" Nate had gotten on the freeway, and he was looking at Vince in the rearview mirror.

"Nate, tell him."

"She's right. About everything. This week has been tough, but it gets a lot worse. There's no guarantee you'll make it out alive."

"I know that," Vince said. "I've thought about it. And if you'll have me, I've made my choice."

"It's okay with me. You're a good man, and we need that on our team."

"Nate!"

"He asked. I'm just telling the truth."

She turned back to Vince. "I wouldn't be able to take it if something happened to you."

"Then we'll make sure nothing does."

"Your mother's house... Your house."

"I've got it covered. I've let the real estate agent know I'll be out of the country. She's got people who'll pack everything and put it in storage. Once she sells the house, she'll hold the money until we figure out how to get it safely."

"That's your money."

"No. It's *our* money. I know you're hurting, and tonight's been a bitch, but pay attention." He grinned. "I love you. I'm not letting you face this crap alone. I'm in. For the duration. Got it?"

She stared at him with her eyes wide open. He was walking into hell…for her. Because he loved her. Her eyes burned and her body ached and she'd almost been killed several times, yet all she could think was that she was so incredibly lucky.

"Well?" he asked.

"I love you, too," she said.

"Thank God," he said.

Then, pains be damned, she kissed him.

Epilogue

Thirty-two days later...

VINCE GOT THE NEWSPAPER from the front stoop. He checked the area, noting the cars that were parked on the street, looking for anything that seemed out of place. Nothing caught his eyes. He went back inside, bolting the door shut. Kate was in the kitchen, waiting.

He threw the morning edition of the *Times* on the table without looking at the headline.

Kate unfolded the paper. "It's here."

He poured himself another cup of coffee, then went to take his seat next to Kate. She started to read. Vince sipped his coffee as Baker's article unfolded. The reporter had exposed the bastards. He'd done his research well, and Omicron was named. So was Leland Ingram, the man Nate had been bugging all this time. Baker had even called the head of Homeland Security to investigate the gas.

It was huge and it was going to cause shock waves throughout Washington. Throughout the entire nation. And he was pretty damn sure Omicron wasn't going to take it lying down.

"You think there's something on the news?" she asked.

He went over to the small TV on the counter and turned it to CNN. They didn't have to wait long for the uproar. Reporters were outside the storage facility and at Omicron headquarters.

He went back to his seat at their awful kitchen table. This apartment had come furnished, and they hadn't wanted to spend any money on upgrades. So they had stuck a matchbook under the short leg and used a tablecloth so they wouldn't get splinters.

Kate smiled at him, and lifted her coffee mug. They toasted quietly because this was just one step. A big step, yes, but just one.

Vince kissed her, and her smile made him want her. Of course, everything made him want her.

Yeah, it was a crappy apartment, but he didn't give a damn. Not when he got to go to bed with her every night and wake up to her every morning. They lived off his savings as she focused all her energy on the painstaking work of compiling evidence from the ledgers. He spent most of his days working with Nate. Doing intel, following up on leads, tracking people. He knew a hell of a lot more about surveillance than he had before.

But he came home to Kate, and that made up for everything. His mother's house had just sold, and that money would keep them for a while longer. And now this. Baker, that sonofabitch, had come through. On all counts.

Jeff's duplicity had been exposed. Tim's name had been cleared, Purchase House was once again in business. The meth labs had been closed down, and the Wu Chang was no longer a functioning gang in Chinatown.

Seth was healing, but still bitter as hell. From what Vince could see, Harper was taking it well, but she was tired. She still worked in the clinic an ungodly amount of hours, then she came home and worked with Seth. Vince just wished that Seth would ease up on her a bit. She had saved his life.

"What the hell?"

Vince turned his attention back to the TV. Kate went to the counter and cranked up the volume. Senator Jackson Raines from California was holding a press conference, and behind him, on a bulletin board, were pictures of Nate, Seth, Boone and Cade, all of them in uniform.

She came back to the table, and took his hand as the senator spoke. With great fervor and much indignation, he accused the men he'd come to know and respect of being terrorists and traitors. Of trying to sell the poison gas to foreign enemies. And he vowed to the American people that he would stop at nothing to capture and convict each and every one of them.

Kate squeezed Vince's hand. "Now we know who's controlling the money," she said, her voice amazingly calm, considering. "And you know what? He's going to pay. No way in hell this country isn't going to know the truth. That our guys are heroes."

Vince looked at her and was stunned yet again at her grace and courage. "They're not the only heroes."

She kissed him, so hard he had to grab the side of the table. And when she pulled back, there was that stunning determination in her eyes, that flash of fire he knew so well. "We have work to do."

"Yep," he said. "Let's lock and load."

* * * * *

*Look for Seth's story, coming in January 2007.
#301 RELEASE is the second book in the exciting
IN TOO DEEP trilogy by Jo Leigh. Enjoy!*

New York Times *bestselling author*
Linda Lael Miller
is back with a new romance
featuring the heartwarming McKettrick family
from Silhouette Special Edition.

SIERRA'S HOMECOMING
by Linda Lael Miller

On sale December 2006,
wherever Silhouette books are sold.

Turn the page for a sneak preview!

Soft, smoky music poured into the room.

The next thing she knew, Sierra was in Travis's arms, close against that chest she'd admired earlier, and they were slow dancing.

Why didn't she pull away?

"Relax," he said. His breath was warm in her hair.

She giggled, more nervous than amused. What was the matter with her? She was attracted to Travis, had been from the first, and he was clearly attracted to her. They were both adults. Why not enjoy a little slow dancing in a ranch-house kitchen?

Because slow dancing led to other things. She took a step back and felt the counter flush against her lower back. Travis naturally came with her, since they were holding hands and he had one arm around her waist.

Simple physics.

Then he kissed her.

Physics again—this time, not so simple.

"Yikes," she said, when their mouths parted.

He grinned. "Nobody's ever said that after I kissed them."

She felt the heat and substance of his body pressed against hers. "It's going to happen, isn't it?" she heard herself whisper.

"Yep," Travis answered.

"But not tonight," Sierra said on a sigh.

"Probably not," Travis agreed.

"When, then?"

He chuckled, gave her a slow, nibbling kiss. "Tomorrow morning," he said. "After you drop Liam off at school."

"Isn't that…a little…soon?"

"Not soon enough," Travis answered, his voice husky. "Not nearly soon enough."

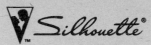

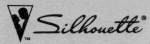

Silhouette®

Romantic
SUSPENSE

From *New York Times*
bestselling author Maggie Shayne

When Selene comes to the aid of an unconscious stranger,
she doesn't expect to be accused of harming him. The
handsome stranger's amnesia doesn't help her cause either.
Determined to find out what really happened to Cory,
the two end up on an intense ride of dangerous pasts
and the search for a ruthless killer.

INTIMATE MOMENTS™

DANGEROUS LOVER #1443
December 2006

Available wherever you buy books.

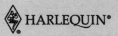

HARLEQUIN®

Blaze™

COMING NEXT MONTH

#291 THE MIGHTY QUINNS: DECLAN Kate Hoffmann
The Mighty Quinns, Bk. 3
Security expert Declan Quinn isn't exactly thrilled with his latest job, acting as bodyguard
for radio sex-pert Rachel Merrell—until she drags him into her bed and shows him what
other things he can do to her body while he's guarding it....

#292 SECRET SANTA Janelle Denison, Isabel Sharpe, Jennifer LaBrecque
(A Naughty but Nice Christmas Collection)
Christmas. Whether it's spending sensual nights cuddled up by the fire or experiencing
the thrill of being caught under the mistletoe by a secret admirer, *anything* is possible at
this time of year. Especially when Santa himself is delivering sexy little secrets....

#293 IT'S A WONDERFULLY SEXY LIFE Hope Tarr
Extreme
Baltimore street cop Mandy Delinski doesn't believe in lust at first sight—at least until
she's almost seduced by gorgeous Josh Thornton at a Christmas party. Talk about a
holiday miracle! For once it looks as if she's going to get *exactly* what she wants for
Christmas—until she finds her "perfect gift" in the morgue the next day....

#294 WITH HIS TOUCH Dawn Atkins
Doing It...Better!
With no notice, Sugar Thompson's business partner Gage Maguire started a seduction
campaign...on *her.* That's against all the rules they established years ago. Sure, he's
tempting her. Only, it's too bad he seems to want more than the temporary fling she has
in mind....

#295 BAD INFLUENCE Kristin Hardy
Sex & the Supper Club II, Bk. 1
Paige Favreau has always taken the safe path. Career, friends, lovers—she's enjoyed them
all, but none have rocked her world. Until blues guitarist Zach Reed challenges her to take
a walk on the wild side....

#296 A TASTE OF TEMPTATION Carrie Alexander
Lust Potion #9, Bk. 3
After a mysterious lust potion works its sexy magic on her pals, gossip columnist
Zoe Aberdeen wants to know the story behind it. When she asks her neighbor—and
crime lab scientist—Donovan Shane for help, he's not interested. But thanks to Zoe's
"persuasive" personality, he's soon testing the potion and acting out his every fantasy
with the sassy redhead....